'MIDNIGHT SONS and the men of Alaska started all this craziness, but the men of Promise refuse to be outdone. They're just as stubborn, just as ornery, just as proud. And just as lovable. Come to Promise—if you're like me, you'll never want to leave!'

Enjoy

Debbie Macomber

Debbie loves to hear from her readers. You can reach her at P.O. Box 1458, Port Orchard, Washington 98366, USA.

THE PEOPLE OF PROMISE:
CAST OF CHARACTERS

Nell Bishop: thirty-something widow with a son, Jeremy, and a daughter, Emma. Her husband died in a tractor accident.

Ruth Bishop: Nell's mother-in-law. Lives with Nell and her two children.

Dovie Boyd: runs an antiques shop and has dated Sheriff Frank Hennessey for ten years.

Caroline Daniels: postmistress of Promise.

Maggie Daniels: Caroline's five-year-old daughter.

Dr. Jane Dickinson: new doctor in Promise.

Ellie Frasier: owner of Frasier's Feed Store.

Frank Hennessey: local sheriff.

Max Jordan: owner of Jordan's Towne & Country.

Wade McMillen: preacher of Promise Christian Church.

Edwina and Lily Moorhouse: sisters. Retired schoolteachers.

Cal and Glen Patterson: local ranchers. Brothers.

Phil and Mary Patterson: parents of Cal and Glen. Operate a local B&B.

Louise Powell: town gossip.

Wiley Rogers: sixty-year-old foreman at the Weston ranch.

Laredo Smith: wrangler hired by Savannah Weston.

Barbara and Melvin Weston: mother and father to Savannah, Grady and Richard. The Westons died six years ago.

Richard Weston: youngest of the Weston siblings.

Savannah Weston: Grady and Richard's sister.

Grady Weston: oldest of the Weston siblings.

DEBBIE MACOMBER

LONE STAR BABY

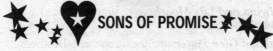 SONS OF PROMISE

MILLS & BOON®

*MILLS & BOON and MILLS & BOON with the Rose Device
are registered trademarks of the publisher.*

*First published in Great Britain 1999
Harlequin Mills & Boon Limited,
Eton House, 18-24 Paradise Road, Richmond, Surrey TW9 1SR*

© Debbie Macomber 1998

ISBN 0 263 81690 7

*Set in Times Roman 10½ on 12 pt.
02-9906-48043 C1*

*Printed and bound in Spain
by Litografia Rosés, S.A., Barcelona*

Chapter One

Amy Thornton was out of money, out of luck and out of hope. Well, she had a little cash left, but her luck had definitely run out, and as for her reserves of hope—they were nonexistent. When the Greyhound bus rolled into the bowling-alley parking lot in Promise, Texas, she stayed in her seat. Disinterested and almost numb, she stared out the window.

Promise seemed like a friendly town. June flower baskets, filled to overflowing with blooming perennials, hung from the streetlights. People stopped to chat, and there was a leisurely, almost festive atmosphere that Amy observed with yearning. Smoke wafted from a barbecue restaurant, and farther down the street, at Frasier Feed, chairs were set up next to a soda machine. A couple of men in cowboy hats and boots sat with their feet propped against the railing; they appeared to find something highly humorous. One of them threw back his head, laughing boisterously. His amusement was contagious and Amy found herself smiling, too.

A couple of people boarded the bus. As soon as they'd taken their seats, the bus doors closed. "Next stop is Brewster," the driver announced.

"Excuse me!" Amy cried, and surprised herself by leaping to her feet. "I want to get off here."

"Here?" The driver looked at her as if he thought he'd misunderstood. The bus had sat there for fifteen minutes without her saying a word.

"Yes," she said, as though Promise had been her destination all along. "I'll need my suitcase."

Muttering irritably under his breath, the driver climbed out of the bus, opened the luggage compartment and extracted her travel-worn case.

Five minutes later, choking on the bus's exhaust, Amy stood in the parking lot, wondering what madness had possessed her. She was homeless, without a job and nearly six months pregnant. She didn't know a soul in this town, yet she felt compelled to start her new life here. Away from her mother. Away from Alex. Away from all the unhappiness that had driven her out of Dallas.

Austin had been her original destination. Her mother's cousin lived there—not that Beverly Ramsey was expecting her. But she *was* the only other family Amy had. Moving to Austin had seemed preferable to staying in Dallas, and despite the pregnancy, she'd felt confident she could find employment fairly quickly, if not in an accounting office, then perhaps as a temp. Anything would do for now, as long as she managed to meet her expenses until she located something more permanent. Naturally she'd hoped that Beverly would invite her to stay until she found an apartment. Two weeks, she'd promised herself. No longer. Just until she was back on her feet. Yet the thought of calling her mother's cousin mortified Amy. Her mother had sponged off Beverly's kindheartedness for years. It went against everything in Amy to ask for help. She'd rather make it on her own.

If only she knew what to do.

Promise, Texas. Holding her suitcase with both hands, she glanced down Main Street again. If ever she'd needed a promise, it was now. A promise and a miracle—or two.

The baby kicked and Amy automatically flattened her hand against her stomach. "I know, Sarah, I know," she whispered to her unborn child. She hadn't had an ultrasound but chose to think of her baby as a girl and had named her Sarah. "It's not the smartest move we've made, is it? I don't know a soul in this town, but it looks like the kind of place where we could be happy."

Her stomach growled and she tried to remember the last time she'd eaten. A small poster advertising $1.99 breakfast special showed in the bowling-alley window. Apparently there was a café inside.

The small restaurant was busy; almost all the seats were taken, but Amy was fortunate to find an empty booth. A waitress handed her a menu when she brought her a glass of water and glanced at her suitcase.

"You miss the bus, honey?" she asked. "You need a place to wait?"

"Actually I just got off," Amy said, touched by the other woman's concern. "I'll take the breakfast special."

"It's the best buy in town," the woman, whose name tag identified her as Denise, said as she wrote the order down on her pad.

Seeing that the waitress was the friendly sort, Amy asked, "Do you happen to know of someone who needs a competent bookkeeper?"

Denise gnawed thoughtfully on her lip. "I can't say I do, but I'm sure there's a job for you in Promise if you're planning to settle here."

The news cheered Amy as much as the welcome she felt. Already she was beginning to believe she'd made the right decision. Promise, Texas, would be her new address—the town where she'd raise her baby. Where she'd make a life for them both. "I can do just about anything," Amy added, not bothering to disguise her eagerness, "and I'm not picky, either."

"Then I'm sure all you need to do is ask around."

A rancher sitting at a table across from Amy caught Denise's eye and lifted his empty coffee mug. "Be right with you, Cody," she said, then looked back at Amy. "Tex will have your meal out in a jiffy."

"Thanks for your help," Amy said, grateful for Denise's encouragement and kindness. As she waited, she found herself fighting the urge to close her eyes. She staved off a yawn as her meal arrived.

The eggs, toast and hash browns tasted better than anything she'd ever eaten. She hadn't realized how hungry she was and had to force herself to eat slowly. When she'd finished the meal, Amy left her money on the table and included a larger than usual tip in appreciation for Denise's welcoming helpfulness.

As she stood up to leave, the rancher Denise had called Cody sent her a curious glance. He smiled in her direction until he noticed the slight rounding of her abdomen, then his eyes widened and he abruptly turned the other way. Amy shook her head in amusement.

Taking Denise's advice, she walked down Main Street and looked for Help Wanted signs posted in store windows. She saw none, and it occurred to her that it might not be a good idea to apply for a position, suitcase in hand. Her first priority was finding a place to live. Besides, her feet hurt and the suitcase was getting heavier by the minute.

That was when Amy saw the church. It could have appeared on a postcard. Small and charming, it was built of red brick and had wide, welcoming steps that led up to arched double doors. They were open, and although she felt silly thinking this, the church seemed to be inviting her in.

Amy soon found herself walking toward it. Lugging her suitcase up the stairs, she entered the vacant church and looked around. The interior was dark on one side, while rainbow-hued sunlight spilled in through stained-glass windows on the other.

Silently she stepped inside, slipped into a back pew and sat down. It felt good to be off her feet and she gave an audible sigh, followed by a wide yawn. She'd rest a few minutes, she decided. Just a few minutes…

The male voice that reached her came out of nowhere. Amy bolted upright. Her eyes flew open and she realized she'd fallen asleep in the pew.

"I beg your pardon," she said, instantly feeling guilt. It took her a moment to discern anything in the dim interior. When her eyes had adjusted, she saw a tall rugged-looking man standing in the church aisle, staring down at her. He resembled a rancher, not unlike the one she'd seen in the café, except that he wore a suit and a string tie.

"Is there a problem?" he asked, his voice gentle.

"No." She shook her head. "None." Flustered, she stood clumsily and grabbed for her suitcase.

"My sermons might be boring, but people generally wake up before Thursday afternoon." His smile unnerved her.

"I didn't mean to fall asleep. I closed my eyes and the next thing I knew, you were here." She glanced at her watch; she'd drifted off for at least twenty minutes, although it felt more like twenty seconds.

"You don't have anything to apologize for," the man told her kindly. "Are you sure there isn't anything I can do to help?"

"How about a miracle or two?" She hadn't meant to sound so flippant.

"Hey," he said, dazzling her with a wide Texas grin, "it just so happens miracles are my specialty." He held his arms open as if to say all she needed to do was ask and he'd direct her request to a higher power.

Amy looked more closely at this man, wondering if he was real.

"Wade McMillen," he said, offering her his hand. "Reverend Wade McMillen."

"Amy Thornton." She shook hands with him and withdrew hers quickly.

"Now, what kind of miracle do you need?" he asked, as if rescuing damsels in distress was all part of a day's work.

"Since you asked," Amy said, slowly releasing her breath. "How about a place to live, a job and a father for my baby?"

"Hmm." Reverend McMillen's gaze fell to her stomach. "That might take some doing."

So he hadn't noticed the pregnancy before, but he did now. "Some miracles are harder than others, I guess." Amy shrugged, figuring it was unlikely he'd be able to help her. But she got into this predicament on her own, and she'd get out of it the same way.

"But none are impossible," Wade reminded her. "Come with me."

"Where are we going?"

"The church office. I'll need to ask you a few questions, but as I said, miracles are my specialty."

DOVIE BOYD HENNESSEY stepped back from the display she'd been working on and studied it with a discerning eye. The pine desk was a heavy old-fashioned one. She'd placed a book next to the lamp, with an overturned pair of old wire-rimmed spectacles on top. A cable-knit sweater was casually draped over the back of the chair, as if someone was about to return. The knickknacks, a quill pen and ink bottle along with a couple of framed pictures gave it a well-used comfortable feeling.

The effect was all she'd hoped for. Her shop had enjoyed a rush of business in the past few months, and the antiques were moving almost as fast as she could get them in the door. Just last week she'd sold a solid cherry four-poster bed that had been in inventory for the better part of eighteen months. Dovie was thrilled. Not just because of the sale, but with the bed gone, an entire corner of the shop would be freed up, allowing her to create a brand-new scene.

Designing these homey nooks was what she loved best. If she'd been thirty-five years younger, she'd go back to school and study to be an interior decorator. Her skills were instinctive, and she loved assembling furniture and various bits and pieces to create the illusion of cozy inviting rooms. But with Frank talking about retiring and the two of them traveling, she probably wouldn't be as involved in the running of her store as she'd been in years past.

As if the thought had conjured up the man, the bells above her door chimed and Sheriff Frank Hennessey walked into the shop.

"Frank!" She brightened at the sight of him. They'd been married nine months now—and he could still fluster her! He was a striking man for sixty, handsome and easy on the eye.

"Travis Grant come for that cherry bed yet?"

"Not yet," Dovie told him, wondering at the question.

Frank smiled—and it was a saucy sexy smile she knew all to well. "Frank, don't be ridiculous."

"We're married, aren't we?"

"It's the middle of the afternoon—good heavens, someone could walk in that door any minute." She edged protectively to the other side of the desk.

"You could always lock the door."

"Frank! Be sensible."

He walked toward the desk.

Giggling like a schoolgirl, Dovie moved beyond his reach. "What about the display windows?"

"Draw the shades."

He had an answer for everything.

"Frank, people of our age don't do this sort of thing!"

"Speak for yourself, woman," he said, racing around the desk.

Dovie let out a squeal and fled with her husband in hot pursuit. He'd just about caught up with her when the bells above the door chimed. Frank and Dovie both froze in their tracks.

Louise Powell, the town gossip, stood just inside the doorway staring as if she'd caught them buck naked on the bed. Her head fell back, her mouth dropped open and her eyes grew round as golf balls.

"Well, I never," she began.

"Maybe you should," Frank suggested. "I bet Paul would appreciate a little hanky-panky now and then."

Dovie elbowed her husband in the ribs and heard him swallow a groan. "Is there something I can help you find?" Dovie asked with as much poise as she could muster. A loose curl fell across her forehead and she blew it away, then tucked it back in place.

"I...I came to browse," Louise muttered. "It's Tammy Lee's birthday next week and..."

Dovie couldn't imagine there being anything in this store that Tammy Lee Killenborn would find to her liking. The inventory included classy pieces of jewelry, subtly elegant clothing and delicate figurines. Nothing she sold had sequins—which was more Tammy Lee's style—but Dovie would never have said so.

"I think it might be best if I came back another time," Louise said, mouth pursed in disapproval. She marched out of the store.

Dovie turned to glare at her husband. "You can bet that five minutes from now everyone in town is going to know my husband's a sex fiend."

Frank grinned as though nothing would please him more.

"Have you no shame?" she asked, but had a difficult time holding in a smile.

Her husband took one look at her and burst out laughing.

Dovie soon joined him.

He locked his arms around her and hugged her close. In all her life Dovie had never been loved like this. For twenty-six years she'd been married to Marvin Boyd; while she'd loved him she hadn't experienced this kind of happiness.

"I don't think you need to worry that Louise will return," Frank assured her. "She isn't going to find something for Tammy Lee here—because, my beautiful wife, you don't sell Texas trash."

"Frank, be kind." Dovie's own opinions made her no less guilty, but she was unwilling to confess as much.

"Hey, I'm just being honest."

Dovie went to the small kitchen off the Victorian Tea Room and reached for two mugs. "Do you have time for coffee?"

Frank nodded. "Actually, I have a reason for stopping by."

"You mean other than seducing me in the middle of the day?"

His grin was full of roguish humor. "Wade McMillen phoned a little while ago."

The pastor was a favorite of Dovie's, and Frank's, too. It'd been Wade who'd suggested a solution to their dilemma. As a lifelong bachelor, Frank had feared he was too set in his ways for marriage, but Dovie had found it impossible to continue their relationship without the emotional security and commitment of wedding vows.

Wade had come up with the idea of their getting married but maintaining separate households.

In the months since their wedding Frank had been gradually spending more and more of his evenings with her. In recent weeks the nights he slept at his own house had become few and far between. He'd lived exclusively with her for most of a month now and showed no signs of leaving, although the option was available to him. Once or twice a week, he'd stop off for his mail or an item of clothing, and he'd check on the house, but that was about it.

"Wade's helping an unwed mother who needs a place to live and I think we can help out."

"Us?" Dovie asked. Frank was by nature generous, although few people realized it.

"I had an idea," he said with a thoughtful look, watching her, "but I wanted to talk it over with you first."

"Of course."

Frank carried their coffee to one of the tables, and she followed with a small plate of freshly baked peanut-butter cookies. She noticed her husband's hesitation.

"Frank?"

"I did a background check on this woman. She's clean. I was able to talk to her landlord and her former employer. From everything they said, she's responsible, hardworking and decent. Her employer said her ex-boyfriend was a jerk. Apparently he hounded her day and night, insisting she get an abortion. From the sound of it, he made life so uncomfortable she quit her job and told everyone she was moving in with family."

"Where's her family, then?"

Frank's gaze held Dovie's. "From what I could find out, she doesn't have anyone to speak of her. Her mother's a flake, her father's dead and apparently that's just about all there is."

"The poor thing."

"I was thinking…" Frank hesitated. "My house has been sitting empty the last month and, well, it probably wouldn't hurt to have someone house-sit. I don't need the rent money, and it'd be a help to me, too."

It took Dovie a moment to understand what he was telling her. "You want to move in permanently with me?"

"For all intents and purposes, I'm living with you now," he said. "There's fewer and fewer of my things at the house. Some old clothes and my furniture. But I won't do it, Dovie, if you object, although I'd like to help Wade and this woman if I could."

"Object?" She all but threw herself into his arms. "Frank, I'm positively delighted!"

"You are?"

She couldn't have hidden her happiness for anything. "I love having you live with me."

"I'd like to keep my house."

"Of course."

"But if it's going to sit empty ninety percent of the time, it makes sense to have someone living there."

"I couldn't agree with you more." This was better than she'd hoped, better than she'd dreamed.

"Naturally, it's only on a trial basis."

"You could move back to your own place anytime, Frank, you know that."

"I wanted to talk to you about it first, but it does seem that letting this young lady stay at the house would help her *and* me. It's a win-win situation."

"It does seem like that, doesn't it?" He sounded as though he'd thought this through but wanted her either to concur or talk him out of it. "Are you sure you're comfortable having a stranger live in your home?"

"Why not? Anything of value has long since gone to your place."

"Our place," she corrected softly. "My home is your home. You're my husband." She said the word with pride and a heart full of love. For eleven years they'd dated and during that time he'd come to her back door. Twice a week, regular as taxes. As her husband, there was no need for him to worry about avoiding gossip, no need to conceal his love. No reason for her to pretend, either.

"And you're my wife." He clasped her hand and squeezed gently.

"Do you want to call Wade now?"

"I think I will." He scooped up a couple of peanut-butter cookies and headed toward her office in the back of the store.

Dovie took a cookie and relaxed in her chair. She had yet to meet this young woman of Wade's, but she liked her already. This unwed mother had helped Frank make a decision he might otherwise have delayed for months—if not years.

WADE HAD BEEN JOKING when he told Amy Thornton he was a miracle worker. But it was clear from the moment he saw her that she was in serious distress. Her face was drawn and her large dark eyes were ringed with shadows. When he found her in the church, she'd looked embarrassed and apologetic. Before he could stop her, she'd grabbed her suitcase and clung to it like a lifeline.

Wade persuaded her to come into the office, where he introduced her to his secretary, Martha Kerns. While the women talked, he made several discreet phone calls from his study. He heard Martha suggest a cup of herbal tea, and a few minutes later her footsteps as she left the room. Interrupting his phone calls, Wade peeked out the door to see how Amy was doing. To his surprise, she was sound asleep, leaning to one side, head resting against her shoulder, eyes closed.

As unobtrusively as possible, he lifted her feet onto the sofa and she nestled against a pillow. He paused to study her. In the short walk from the church to the office, she'd told him she was twenty-five, a full eight years younger than he was. Never had eight years seemed so wide a gulf. She was pretty, with thick shoulder-length auburn hair, pulled back and clipped in place. Her skin was naturally pale and wonderfully smooth. Had he touched her cheek, he was certain she would have felt like satin.

Martha returned from the kitchen with two mugs and set them down on the corner of her desk. "She looks a little like an angel, doesn't she?"

Wade didn't answer, but not because he didn't agree. Amy did indeed look angelic. Removing his sweater from his closet, he covered the sleeping woman's shoulders.

While Amy continued to doze, he made a few more phone calls and finally managed to reach Frank Hennessey. Within the hour Frank called him back.

"I'm over at Dovie's," the sheriff announced. "We

think we've come up with a solution to the housing problem.''

"You know of someone willing to give her a place to live for a few months?'' Wade's original thought had been to hook her up with one of the local ranchers as a cook or other part-time helper, but he'd soon realized that her pregnancy would restrict her activities. From there his thoughts moved to the idea of her working as a live-in nanny. In March Savannah Smith had delivered a beautiful baby girl, and Caroline Weston was due in three or four months. Weddings and babies. Wade had been witness to them all.

"Actually I was thinking she might be willing to house-sit for a while.''

"Excellent idea.'' Wade wished he'd thought of that himself. "But who?''

Frank cleared his throat. "Uh, Dovie and I talked it over, and we were thinking maybe she could watch my place.''

It didn't take Wade long to understand the implications. "That's an excellent idea,'' he said again.

"I did a background check on her,'' Frank said. "Talked to her former employer, too. From everything he said, she's a good person who's been put in a difficult position.''

"I don't know what she can afford for rent.''

"I don't plan on charging her any,'' the sheriff said. "She'd be doing me and Dovie a favor. Besides, she has other expenses to worry about.''

"That's very kind of you,'' Wade said. So Frank had made inquiries concerning Amy. It was all Wade could do not to interrogate him. Sleeping Beauty was in his outer office, and he wanted to know more about her. *Much* more. She didn't fit the homeless helpless mode. He wondered why she'd decided to come here, where she had no friends or relatives, no prospects of work or accommodation.

"I have a line on a job for her," Wade said, feeling downright proud of himself.

"Wonderful. Who?"

"Ellie Frasier," he said, forgetting that the feed-store owner was a Patterson now. Glen and Ellie were married last September; he'd officiated at the ceremony himself.

"The feed store?" Frank didn't sound as if he approved of the idea.

"As a bookkeeper," Wade told him. "I told Ellie up front that she's pregnant, but she didn't seem to mind. Ellie said she'd like to meet Amy first and interview her. She's been looking for someone to come in part-time and take up the slack. She could occasionally use help in the store, too." Wade was beginning to feel like the miracle worker he'd confidently proclaimed himself to be. He grinned, thinking all his miracles should be this easy.

"Dovie and I would like to meet her, too."

"Of course." It stunned him that Frank would open his home to a stranger like this. Frank and Dovie knew next to nothing about Amy Thornton, other than what her former employer had said. Yet they felt comfortable enough to invite her to live in his house. Wade wasn't sure he would've been as generous or as trusting. However, Frank was a lawman—a sheriff who'd seen plenty of reason to distrust his fellow man—and if he trusted Amy, Wade could do no less.

They ended the conversation by arranging that Wade would bring her over to the shop in an hour or so.

Wade returned to the outer room. Amy stirred then and sat up, looking disoriented, as if she wasn't sure where she was. "Oh, my," she whispered, pushing the hair away from her face. "I'm so sorry. I don't know what's wrong with me. I…I can't seem to get enough sleep."

"Don't worry about it," Wade said, and Martha added, "You need extra sleep right now."

"There are some people I'd like you to meet," Wade told her.

"I don't mean to cause you a lot of problems, Reverend McMillen," she said as she handed him his sweater.

"You're not a problem, Amy. Besides, didn't I tell you miracles were my specialty?"

"Fortunately Mr. Miracle Worker here has a lot of helpers in the community," Martha said with a smile.

Wade couldn't have agreed with her more. He led Amy out of the office and to the curb where he'd parked his Blazer. A soft breeze rustled the leaves of maples and oaks, the faint scent of roses and jasmine perfumed the air.

"I'm taking you to Dovie's place first," Wade said, starting the engine. "Frank and Dovie wanted to meet you—and discuss an idea."

"An idea?"

"I'll let them explain."

The Hennesseys were waiting for them. He watched Amy's face when she walked into Dovie's antique store. She paused as if it was too much to assimilate. He'd felt much the same way when he'd first seen the sheer *number* of things in her store. He'd been impressed by Dovie's displays, though. They were so attractive he couldn't help feeling they belonged in a magazine. When she opened her Victorian Tea room, it'd fast become the gathering place for women all around town. Dovie used only the finest linens, the best crystal and bone china from her stock. At first Wade had felt as awkward in her store as he would in a lingerie shop, but Dovie had quickly put him at ease.

"You must be Amy," Dovie said, crossing the room to greet them. "Welcome to my shop."

"It's...beautiful." Amy couldn't stop looking around.

"I've made us tea," Dovie said, and they followed her to a table at the far side of the room.

Frank watched Amy carefully and Wade saw her meet his gaze without flinching or visible discomfort. He sensed she had nothing to hide, and for that Wade was grateful. Situations such as this held the risk of problems; one of his fears was that Amy was running away, possibly from the father of her unborn child. But despite the potential for trouble, he wanted to help her.

Frank waited until everyone had a cup of tea before he mentioned his idea.

"You mean to say you'd let me live in your home?" Amy sounded incredulous. "But you don't even know me."

"Are you hiding something? Is there anything in your background we should know?" Frank asked.

"No," she was quick to inform them, her eyes wide and honest.

"I didn't think so." Frank's features relaxed into an easy smile. "Actually, having you stay there helps us, too. I won't need to worry about the house sitting empty, and you'll have a place to live until you've sorted out your life and made some decisions."

"I...I don't know what to say other than thank you."

Wade could see that Amy was overwhelmed by the Hennesseys' generosity and trust.

"I won't disappoint you," she said as if making a pledge.

"Just so you'll know exactly what's expected of you, I thought we should sit down and put everything in writing. I don't want there to be room for any misunderstanding."

"I'd like that," Amy concurred.

"Do you want to see the house?"

"Please."

Wade stood and checked his watch. "Give us thirty minutes. Amy needs to talk to Ellie first."

"Fine, I'll see you then."

Wade escorted Amy out of the shop and down the street to Frasier Feed. Ellie's father had died the year before, and Ellie had taken over the business. He knew that Glen had been helping her with the paperwork, but it had become an increasingly onerous task. Ellie was finding that it required more time than she could spare.

Ellie met them on the sidewalk outside the store.

"This is Amy Thornton," Wade said, introducing the two women. "Amy, Ellie Patterson."

"Hi," Ellie said, her greeting friendly. She gestured to the chairs by the soda machine. They all sat down, although Wade wasn't sure he was really needed for this interview.

"If you don't mind, I have a few questions," Ellie said.

"All right." Amy stiffened a little, as though unsure what to expect.

Ellie asked about job experience and Wade was glad of the opportunity to listen in. He was pleased to learn Amy had worked for the same employer for almost seven years. She'd started with the company as part of a high-school training program and had stayed on after graduation.

Wade remembered Frank telling him that her former employer had given her a glowing recommendation.

"Seven years." Ellie seemed impressed. She asked a series of other questions and took down references and phone numbers. Wade watched in amazement as almost instant rapport developed between the two women.

"Could you start on Monday?" Ellie asked.

"You're offering me the job?" Amy's voice quavered. "Now? Already?"

"Does that surprise you?"

"I'm...shocked. And thrilled. Thank you. Thank you so much." Tears gathered in her eyes and she stopped for a moment to compose herself before she continued. "Your store," she said, having a hard time getting the words out. "It's one of the reasons I got off the bus."

"I don't understand," Ellie said.

"It looked so friendly, like your customers were also your friends."

"My customers *are* my friends," Ellie said. "I'm hoping we can become friends, too."

A smile lit up Amy's face. "I'd like that very much."

Wade grinned in delight. This was working out perfectly. Within hours of arriving in Promise, Amy Thornton had a job and a place to live. Frank, Dovie and Ellie reaffirmed his belief in the basic goodness of most people.

Once they were back in the car, Wade drove to Frank's house and pulled into the driveway.

Amy glanced at him. "This is the house?"

Actually it was more of a cottage, Wade thought. Cozy and comfortable-looking.

"You really are a miracle worker, aren't you?" she said in apparent awe.

"A place to live and a job. Hey, no problem," he said, snapping his fingers like a magician producing a rabbit in a hat. "No problem at all."

"I don't think finding a father for my baby is going to be as easy," she said, climbing out of the vehicle.

A father for her child. Wade had forgotten about that.

Chapter Two

Dr. Jane Patterson had a gentle way about her, Amy thought as she dressed. The examination had been her most comfortable to date. From the moment she learned she was pregnant, Amy had faithfully taken her vitamins, made regular doctor's appointments and scrupulously watched her diet. Her one fear was that her baby would feel the tension and stress that had been her constant companion these past six months.

There was a light tap on the door, and Dr. Patterson entered the examination room.

"Is everything all right with the pregnancy?" Amy asked immediately.

"Everything looks good. From what I could tell, the baby is developing right on schedule," Dr. Patterson said. "I don't want you to worry. Continue with the vitamins and try to get the rest your body needs." She sat down across from Amy, leaned forward and gave her a reassuring pat on the hand. "I'm going to be starting a birthing class in the next couple of weeks and was wondering if you'd care to join."

Amy bit her lip. She'd like nothing better than to attend this class, but it probably required a partner, someone who'd be willing to coach her through labor and birth.

Unfortunately, being new in town, she didn't know anyone she could ask.

"There are several women in the community who are entering their third trimester," the doctor went on.

"Will I need a partner?"

"It's not necessary," she said, and Amy saw compassion and understanding on the doctor's face. "You don't need to decide just yet," she added. "As I mentioned, the class won't start for a couple of weeks, but if you're looking for a partner, I suggest you ask Dovie Hennessey. She took me under her wing when I first arrived in Promise. I didn't know anyone and had trouble making friends."

"You?" Amy could hardly believe it.

Dr. Patterson laughed lightly. "Oh, Amy, you wouldn't believe all the mistakes I made. I felt so lost and lonely. Dovie made me feel welcome and steered me toward the right people. She's wonderful."

Amy lowered her gaze, embarrassed that she was reduced to accepting charity and relying on the kindness of strangers. "Did you know I'm staying in Sheriff Hennessey's house?" she asked.

"I heard you're house-sitting, if that's what you mean."

It puzzled Amy that she could have stepped off the bus in a town she didn't know existed and be welcomed as though she were long-lost family. Half the time she was left wondering when she'd wake up to reality. Wade McMillen had jokingly said he was a miracle worker, and so far, he'd proved himself to be exactly that. A week later, her head still spun at the way he'd gone about finding solutions to her problems.

"Would you like me to put your name down for the birthing class?" Dr. Patterson pressed.

"Yes, please," Amy said. It seemed that the people of Promise, Texas, had made room for her in their community and in their hearts. "I'll think about asking Dovie..." She hated to request yet another favor. Besides, she couldn't see what would prompt a busy woman like Dovie to agree, especially when she and her husband were already doing so much for her. Dr. Patterson seemed to think it was a good idea, though, and Amy wouldn't mind becoming friends with the older woman. Everyone she knew was back in Dallas. Her friends, her colleagues and of course her mother. Alex hadn't liked her seeing anyone else, even girlfriends, and over time she'd lost contact with quite a few people.

"Dovie will be thrilled if you ask her," the doctor was saying.

Amy stared at her. "Dr. Patterson, I don't know—"

"We don't stand on formality here," the other woman interrupted. "You can call me Jane—Dr. Jane if you prefer." The accompanying smile was warm.

"You'll let me know when the classes start?"

"Jenny has the sign-up sheet out front. Give her your name and she'll make sure you're notified before the first class. And while you're speaking to Jenny, go ahead and schedule your next appointment for two weeks."

"Two weeks?" The doctor in Dallas had seen her only once a month. "There's something wrong you're not telling me about, isn't there?"

"Relax, Amy, everything looks perfectly fine. You're healthy and there's nothing to indicate anything's wrong with the baby."

"Then why?"

"You're entering the third trimester, and it's normal procedure to see a patient every two weeks until the last month, when your visits will be weekly."

Amy relaxed. Generally she didn't panic this easily, but

so much had already happened that she couldn't help worrying.

"I'll talk to Jenny on my way out," she promised.

"If you have any questions, I want you to call me day or night, understand?" Jane wrote the office phone number on a prescription pad and handed it to Amy. "This is my pager number if the office is closed and it's not an emergency."

"Thank you." Amy's voice shook. She felt overwhelmed by the fact that strangers cared about her and her unborn child when her own mother's reaction had been just the opposite. She'd called Amy ugly horrible names. Alex, the man she was convinced she loved beyond life itself, had shown exactly the kind of person he was when she told him about the baby. He didn't want his own child! People she loved, trusted, had turned their backs on her, and instead a community of strangers had welcomed her with open arms, taken her in, given her the help she needed.

"You'll talk to Dovie then?" Jane said as Amy prepared to leave.

Amy inhaled a stabilizing breath and nodded. "I'll do it right away." Before she lost her nerve or changed her mind.

Since she wasn't expected at the feed store until noon, Amy walked over to Dovie's after she'd left the doctor's office. She tried to convince herself that what Jane had said was true—that Dovie would be delighted to attend the classes with her.

Birthing classes. In three months Sarah would be born. Three months! This shouldn't have come as any shock. But it did. She had so much to do to get ready for the baby. She hadn't even begun to buy the things she'd need. Baby clothes, a crib, a stroller. Her heart started to pound at the thought of everything that had to be done and the short time left in which to accomplish it all.

Amy pushed open the door to Dovie's store and the bells above the entrance jingled lightly.

"Well, hello, Amy," Dovie greeted her from across the room. She was arranging freshly cut red roses in a crystal vase. "Aren't these lovely?" she murmured, pausing to examine one bud more closely. "Savannah Smith came by with Laura earlier this morning and brought me these."

"They're beautiful." Amy swore that if Dovie hadn't been alone just then, she would have abandoned her mission.

"How are you feeling?" Dovie asked.

"Great. I'm enjoying working with Ellie."

"From what Ellie said, you're doing a fabulous job."

Amy was unable to stifle a smile. She'd started her job that Monday afternoon and had spent the first two days organizing Ellie's desk. It was abundantly clear that Ellie had been putting off too much of her paperwork. This job wasn't a fabricated one; Amy was convinced of that. Frasier Feed genuinely needed a bookkeeper and more. Her organizational skills had given her the opportunity to show Ellie how much she appreciated the job.

"Ellie's a wonderful employer."

"After your first day she told me she wondered why she'd delayed hiring someone."

Amy had wondered that herself, but didn't think it was her place to ask. If anything, she was grateful Ellie had waited; otherwise there wouldn't have been an opening for her.

"I just finished seeing Dr. Patterson for the first time," Amy said.

"Isn't Jane terrific?" Dovie's question was asked in an absent sort of way, more comment than inquiry. She added another perfectly formed long-stemmed rose to the arrangement.

"Yes... She mentioned she's starting a birthing class in a couple of weeks."

"Caroline Weston's due around the same time as you."

Amy wasn't entirely sure who Caroline was. A friend of Dovie's apparently.

"I'm going to need a birthing partner," Amy blurted out, thinking if she didn't ask soon, she never would. "Dr. Patterson...Dr. Jane assured me I could attend the class alone, but then she suggested I ask you to be my partner." She dragged a deep breath into her lungs and hurriedly continued, "I realize it's an imposition and I want you to know that I..." She let her sentence drift off.

Dovie's hand stilled and she glanced up, her eyes wide. With astonishment? Or perhaps it was shock; Amy didn't know which. Her initial reaction had been accurate. Asking something this personal of someone she barely knew, someone who'd already helped her so much, was stepping over the line.

"An imposition," Dovie repeated. "Oh, no, not to me. Not at all. I'd consider it an honor."

"You would? I mean, Dovie, you and Frank have done so much for me and the baby. Letting me stay in his house... I can't tell you how grateful I am. Thank you. Thank you." If she didn't leave soon, Amy feared she'd embarrass herself further by bursting into tears.

"Just let me know when the first class is scheduled, all right?"

Amy nodded. "Jenny said she'd have all the information for me at my next appointment."

"We'll make a great team." Dovie's eyes gleamed with confidence; she gave every indication of being delighted that Amy had asked her. Just like Dr. Jane had said.

Amy had almost stopped believing there were good people left in this world, and then she'd stumbled on a whole town of them.

DENISE PARSONS HAD NEVER BEEN friendly with Louise Powell. The woman enjoyed gossip and meddling far too much. The minute Louise entered the café, Denise could tell she wanted something—and she sincerely doubted it was the French-dip luncheon special.

Sighing with resignation, Denise filled a glass of water and reached for a menu, then approached the booth.

"Hello, Denise," the other woman purred.

Yup, she was after some juicy gossip all right, but Denise hadn't a clue what it might be. Well, whatever Louise hoped to learn had brought her into the bowling alley on a Thursday afternoon, which was highly unusual.

"Hello." She returned the greeting with a certain hesitation. She didn't enjoy being a party to Louise's type of friendship. "What can I get you?"

"Coffee would be great."

"Would you like anything with that?" Tex had been after her to push desserts. With one of the ranchers she might have suggested a slice of rhubarb pie, but personally she preferred to have Louise in and out of the café in record time.

"I understand you were the first one to speak with that new gal in town," Louise said, instead of answering Denise's question.

Denise wasn't sure who she meant.

"The pregnant one."

So Amy Thornton was the reason for this visit. Denise hadn't noticed Amy was pregnant until she'd stood up to leave. Louise stared at her, anticipating an answer. "Yes, I talked to her." She couldn't see any point in denying it.

"Did you say you wanted anything with the coffee?" she asked again.

"Nothing." Louise righted her mug and gazed up expectantly.

Denise wasn't about to let the town busybody trap her into a lengthy and unpleasant conversation; she promptly disappeared. She was back a minute later with the coffeepot and a look that suggested she didn't have anything more to add.

Oblivious to anything but her own curiosity, Louise was ready and waiting. "What did she say?"

"Who?" Denise asked, playing dumb.

"That unwed mother," Louise snapped.

"She asked about the breakfast special."

Louise's eyes narrowed. "Did she mention the baby's father?"

Setting the coffeepot down on the table, Denise leaned closer as though to share a secret. "She did say something interesting."

The rhinestones in the older woman's hat sparkled as she scooted closer to the end of the booth. "What?"

"She asked…" Denise paused and looked both ways. *"What?"*

"If we served sourdough bread."

The keen interest in Louise's eyes changed to annoyance. Her back went stiff and she straightened, moving away from Denise, implying that it didn't do her image any good to be seen associating with a waitress. "I can see we have nothing more to discuss," Louise said primly. "And furthermore, this coffee tastes burned."

"I made a fresh pot less than thirty minutes go." Denise had a son in junior high, a kid with attitude. If she wanted someone to insult her and question her abilities, she could get it at home; she didn't need to go to work for it.

With her lips pinched, Louise scrambled out of the booth. She slapped some change down on the table and walked out the door, leaving it to swing in her wake.

"What'd that old biddy want?" Tex shouted from the kitchen.

"She's trying to make trouble, is all." Denise put the coffeepot back on the burner. "Asking about Amy." The unwed mother was fair game in Louise's eyes, Denise realized sadly. The poor girl was doing the best she could and Denise hoped everything would work out well for her and her baby.

"Did you tell her leave the kid alone?" Tex demanded, none too gently.

"I did," Denise shouted back. In her own way she'd given Louise as good as she got, and she felt a small but definite sense of triumph.

WADE HAD KNOWN Amy was scheduled to visit Jane on Thursday morning, so he waited until later that evening to visit her. The last time they'd talked had been Sunday morning.

He'd be lying if he didn't admit how pleased he'd felt when Amy showed up for church services. Frankly he'd been more than a little surprised. In his years of serving as a pastor, he'd learned a number of lessons about human nature, not all of them positive—and as a result he'd suffered his share of disappointments. He sincerely hoped Amy wouldn't turn out to be one.

Richard Weston had certainly tested his faith in people. The youngest of the Weston family had shown up in Promise after a six-year absence and taken advantage of the kindness and goodwill of the community. Just when his underhandedness was about to be exposed, he'd disappeared. Eventually he was found—hiding in a nearby ghost town—and returned to New York to stand trial on charges stemming from a scheme that had involved cheating and abusing immigrants. Wade had spent many an evening with Grady Weston and his sister, Savannah Smith, helping them come to terms with what their brother had done—to them and to others. Richard was serving a twenty-five-year prison sentence, and it was unlikely he'd ever come back to Promise. Not that anyone wanted him to.

His experience working as a pastor had given Wade a sixth sense about people. He'd seen through Richard Weston almost immediately, but unfortunately had been unaware of the man's schemes until too late. Even knowing Richard for what he was, Wade had been shocked by the extent of his perfidy and the horror of his crimes.

He liked Amy and trusted her, not that he was looking for her gratitude. Actually he'd done little more than point her in the right direction. Ellie hadn't hired her simply because she needed a job. And rightly so. She'd hired Amy because of her qualifications.

Home and job—everything had fallen neatly into place. Then on Sunday morning Amy had arrived in time for the morning service, looking almost afraid. Her expressive brown eyes told him she was expecting someone to tell her she should leave. Expecting someone to tell her she didn't belong in a house of God. Wade swore if anyone had so much as tried, he would… He stopped, not realizing until that very moment the depth of his feelings.

He was proud of the way his flock had welcomed Amy Thornton into the fold. Proud of each and every one of them, even Louise, who—so far, anyway—had shown more curiosity than malice.

Wednesday morning Ellie Patterson had phoned Wade to thank him for finding such a whiz of a bookkeeper. Wade couldn't accept full credit; he'd had no idea Amy was a gifted organizer. He smiled, pleased that everything was working out so well.

He rang the doorbell and waited. It might have been best had he phoned first, but he'd learned early on in his pastoral career that if he did phone, most people invented excuses to keep him away. He'd never understood what they feared. Women seemed convinced he'd march right into their kitchens and inspect the inside of their ovens. Men seemed to worry that he might catch them enjoying a bottle of beer—when in reality he'd have been happy to join them.

Involved in these thoughts, Wade stepped back in mild surprise when the door opened and Amy stood on the other side.

"Hello," she said, brightening when she saw who it was.

He wasn't accustomed to people actually being pleased to find he'd unexpectedly dropped by. "I thought I'd see how the doctor's appointment went this morning," he said.

Amy held open the screen door for him. "Come in, please. I just finished making a batch of sun tea. Would you care for a glass?"

"Sure."

Amy had been living at Frank's house for only a week, and already Wade saw subtle changes. She'd draped a shawl over the back of Frank's shabby recliner, and a vase of fresh-cut flowers rested in the center of the coffee table. The wooden floors shone, the windows sparkled; the books were dusted and straightened. A women's magazine lay open on the sofa.

"Make yourself comfortable," she said, and disappeared into the kitchen. She returned a couple of minutes later with two glasses of iced tea. She explained that it was a lemon herbal tea to which she'd added a sprig of fresh mint.

"I hear you were in to see Dr. Jane."

Amy nodded, then sipped from her glass. "She's wonderful."

"We think so."

"I was a little worried, because I was a couple of weeks overdue for an exam, but she assured me the pregnancy is progressing nicely."

Wade noticed how she pressed her palm against her abdomen as she spoke. It was an unconscious movement, he suspected. If he hadn't known about the pregnancy, he probably wouldn't have even guessed her condition. The swelling was slight and could almost be attributed to body type.

"I've signed up for birthing classes and Dovie has agreed to be my partner."

"Dovie," Wade repeated. "That's great." She was a perfect choice. Dovie loved children; a couple of months ago she'd surprised him when she volunteered to teach Sunday-school class for two-and-three-year-olds. What amazed him even more was that Frank had joined his wife one recent Sunday. It'd been difficult enough to get Frank Hennessey to darken a church door—but teaching Sunday school to a group of preschoolers? That had left Wade with his mouth hanging open in shock. Frank Hennessey seemed full of surprises lately, attributable, no doubt, to Dovie's influence. She'd be good for Amy, too, he mused. And vice versa...

"It all seems so real now," Amy was saying. "Dovie seemed pleased about going to the birthing classes with me."

Wade sat back on the sofa. "Have you decided what

you're going to do about the baby?'' he asked. This was a difficult subject, but one that needed to be addressed.

"How do you mean?" Amy asked.

"Have you made any decisions about the baby's future?"

"Are you asking me if I've decided to put my child up for adoption?"

He was pleased she understood his intention without his having to spell it out. This was such a delicate subject. Emotions could be volatile and he wasn't trying to steer her in one direction or another. At twenty-five Amy Thornton was perfectly capable of making up her own mind.

"I'm not here to pressure you in any way," he told her.

"In the beginning I considered all my options." She paused and he saw the muscles in her throat work as she struggled within herself. "The man I loved…who I thought loved me…wanted me to end the pregnancy. My mother, between calling me names, wasn't willing to offer any type of support. She said she wanted nothing to do with me again." Amy regarded him steadily. "Thank you, Wade."

"You're thanking me?"

"You're the first person in nearly six months to ask what I want for my child."

He noticed the sheen in her eyes. "So, what have you decided?"

Her hand went back to her abdomen. "I'm an adult and I have good job skills. Ellie seems to think the part-time position will develop into full-time employment. While I don't have a lot of discretionary income and finances will be tight, I've decided to raise my baby myself."

The decision hadn't been easy, Wade knew. He could tell from the look on her face. She was afraid, vulnerable and alone, but she seemed to have found peace with that. It was everything he needed to know.

"I left Dallas because of my baby," Amy said. "The baby's father...well, let me just say that he's out of my life and there's no possibility we'll get back together." She paused and then, unable to hide the pain in her voice, she whispered, "My mother has disowned me." Her voice grew stronger. "The baby and I are a package deal, and seeing that I've already made two rather unpleasant stands on Sarah's behalf, I figure I'll stick it out for the long haul. I'm very much looking forward to being a mother." This part was added with a smile and something more. Inner peace.

Amy Thornton hadn't come to this decision without struggle, Wade realized. It wasn't one she'd made lightly.

"I don't understand the question, though," she said, her mood abruptly shifting into amusement.

"What do you mean?"

"I thought you were the miracle man, Reverend McMillen."

"Well, yes...I suppose, but..."

"Don't go backing out on me now," she said, placing her hand on her hip in mock outrage. "The first time we met, you made it quite clear that you were capable of producing whatever I needed."

"Hey, I found you a house and connected you with Ellie, didn't I?"

"Yes, you did and don't think I'm ungrateful. But if you'll remember, you also promised to find me a father for my baby."

DOVIE POSTED the notice for the big Grange dance in her shop window. Next to the rodeo and chili cook-off, this function, sponsored by the Cattlemen's Association, was one of the biggest social events of the year.

At the dance the previous summer Glen Patterson had made a fool of himself over Ellie. It was one of the incidents that had led—indirectly—to their marriage. Glen had been a little slow to figure out how he felt about Ellie, and Richard Weston had leaped into the breach. Which had helped Glen clarify his own feelings. Certainly Richard was none to happy when Ellie chose to marry Glen, but Dovie strongly suspected Ellie's recent inheritance had been the key to Richard's interest.

Vulnerable as she'd been at the time, it was little wonder Ellie hadn't seen through Richard the minute he started showering her with attention. Eventually she had of course—with no help from Glen, Dovie mused.

She finished taping up the notice for the dance, then stepped outside to make sure it was positioned straight. The day was lovely, the midmorning still cool with a slight breeze. The reader board at the bank alternated the time and the temperature, and Dovie noted it was seventy-four. By late afternoon it'd be close to ninety.

A great many changes had come about since last year's dance. Several marriages, births, including Savannah and Laredo's daughter. Caroline Weston, the town's postmistress and Grady's wife, was showing nicely now and was as pretty as Dovie had ever seen her. She all but glowed with happiness. It wouldn't have surprised Dovie if Ellie or Jane decided to start their families soon, too. Those stubborn Patterson men had waited until their midthirties to get married. Better make up for lost time, Dovie thought with a wicked grin.

"What's that?" Amy Thornton asked, startling her as she walked up behind Dovie and read the sign.

"The Cattlemen's Association puts on a big dance at the Grange hall every year."

"Oh." Amy sounded sorry she'd asked.

"You're going, aren't you?"

Amy shook her head. "Not like this."

"Like what?" Dovie challenged.

The younger woman cradled her protruding stomach. "In case you hadn't noticed, Dovie, I'm six months pregnant."

"What's that got to do with anything?"

Amy shook her head. "I couldn't attend a dance."

"Why not, in heaven's name?"

"I...just couldn't."

"If you're worried about having something appropriate to wear..."

"I don't have anything appropriate, but that's only part of it. I realize these are modern times, but I'd still need a date."

Dovie smiled. "No, you wouldn't. My heavens, plenty of ranchers attend the dance without a partner, and gals, too. Don't you worry, you'll have more men buzzing around you than a can of fresh cream."

"I wouldn't feel...right."

"And why not?" Dovie demanded.

"I...don't know anyone," Amy said.

Dovie studied her for a long minute. "I can't think of a better way for you to get to know the people here, and for them to know you."

Still Amy hesitated.

"Will you at least think on it?" Dovie pressed. Going to the dance was the best way for Amy to meet other people close to her in age. It'd help if she did have someone to escort her, but she was too new in town.

"I'll think about it," Amy said, "but I'm not making any promises."

Dovie patted her elbow, pleased Amy had agreed to at least consider it. "Good girl."

Amy flushed and looked slightly embarrassed. "I wanted you to know that the birthing class starts a week from Monday. We're meeting at the health clinic between seven and eight-thirty."

"I'll be there with bells on," Dovie promised. Excitement bubbled inside her at the prospect of sharing the moment Amy gave birth to her baby.

They exchanged a few more pleasantries, then Amy continued down the street. Feeling motherly, Dovie wandered back into her shop. She'd bonded with Amy Thornton, she thought, nodding in satisfaction. The girl was like a lost waif, in need of love and nourishment. Not physical nourishment, but emotional. Even as little as a week had shown a vast improvement in her appearance. She wasn't nearly as pale, and the dark shadows under her eyes had all but disappeared.

Dovie strongly suspected this was the first time since she'd learned she was pregnant that she was getting proper rest. In thinking over Amy's story, Dovie was appalled. The young woman had hastily gotten off the bus without knowing a soul in Promise. When questioned, all she'd say was that she'd looked down Main Street and thought it might be a friendly town.

While Promise was indeed friendly, it wasn't unlike a dozen other communities Amy had traveled through on her way to Austin.

Dovie wouldn't say anything to Frank, and possibly not even to Wade, but she had the distinct impression that Amy was *supposed* to get off that bus when she did. There was a reason she was in Promise. Dovie wasn't sure what it was just yet, but time would eventually reveal it.

"I can't believe the dance is almost here."

The deep male voice behind her took Dovie by surprise. She gasped and placed her hand over her heart. "Reverend McMillen!"

"Sorry, Dovie, I didn't mean to frighten you."

"I was lost in thought and I didn't hear you sneaking up behind me. Didn't even hear the bell!"

He laughed and handed her the Sunday-school material he'd promised to deliver at the beginning of the week.

"The big dance is scheduled for the twenty-seventh this year," Dovie said. "You're going of course."

"Of course."

Not that Dovie remembered him doing a lot of dancing in years past. Mostly Wade hung around with the ranchers. The thing was, he fit right in. Tall and broad-shouldered, the preacher looked and acted as though he'd be at home on a horse or roping a calf. It often took people aback when they learned the only herd Wade managed was a church full of stubborn humans.

"Remember last year?" Wade asked.

"I'm not likely to forget," Dovie told him.

"Glen was fit to be tied when he found Ellie dancing with Richard."

Dovie had been thinking the same thing herself only a few minutes earlier. "It was a turning point in their relationship."

"Not that the road to romance was smooth for either of them," Wade reminded her.

"The dance was a turning point for Caroline and Grady, too."

This small bit of information appeared to surprise the reverend. "What do you mean?"

"Savannah and I were the ones who encouraged Caroline to ask Grady when Pete Hadley announced a ladies' choice."

"She did, too, didn't she?"

"Yup, and I think that was what woke Grady up to the fact that she's a woman."

Wade rubbed the side of his face. "Seems the dance is responsible for a lot more romances around here than I realized."

That was when the idea hit Dovie—and hit her hard. Actually it was the perfect solution and she wondered why she hadn't come up with it sooner. My, oh my, it *was* just perfect.

"You've got that look in your eye, Dovie," Wade said, and he stepped back warily.

"I do?" she asked, feigning surprise. She'd already concluded that it was no fluke Amy had chosen to settle in Promise, and now she thought she knew why. She blurted out her idea. "I think you should take Amy to the dance."

"Me?" he cried. "Oh, no, you don't! My job description *doesn't* include escorting lonely hearts to dances!"

Chapter Three

Amy stopped at Dovie's house to pick her up for the birthing class far earlier than necessary. She'd been looking forward to this ever since Dr. Jane had first mentioned it. Waiting another fifteen minutes seemed more than she could stand.

Dovie was in her garden when Amy approached.

"Oh, my, is it that time already?" Dovie asked the instant she saw her. Flustered, she glanced at her wrist.

"I'm early," Amy apologized.

"Don't let her kid you," Frank said, joining his wife. "Dovie's been on tenterhooks all evening. I don't think I've ever seen her more excited about anything."

It warmed Amy's heart that her friend was looking forward to coaching her through labor and birth. The thought of having to go through the birth alone had weighed on her mind for months. The wrenching sense of loneliness had virtually disappeared since her arrival in Promise. She marveled anew at these wonderful people.

"I'll just be a moment," Dovie promised, and rushed toward the house.

"There's no hurry," Amy called after her.

Frank sauntered over to the gate and opened it for Amy. "You might as well sit a spell." He led her past the large well-groomed garden toward the wrought-iron table and chairs on the brick patio.

"Dovie's got quite a garden, doesn't she?"

"It's like this every year," the sheriff said. "Heaven only knows what she's going to do with twenty-five tomato plants, but she always seems to know someone who could use them."

Fresh tomatoes were a particular favorite of Amy's. One day she'd like to plant her own garden... Perhaps next year.

"Do you think Dovie would mind if I looked at her plants?" Amy asked, noticing the small herb garden next to the tomatoes.

"Go right ahead. Dovie's garden is her pride and joy. If you want to wait a few minutes, she'll give you the grand tour herself." It seemed to Amy that Frank was just as proud of her accomplishment.

Dovie appeared almost immediately afterward, wearing pressed navy blue trousers and an attractive cotton knit sweater in a lovely rose. Just as Frank had predicted, she was more than willing to walk Amy through her garden. "I seem to have a green thumb," she remarked, shrugging in an offhand way.

"She could coax orchids into blooming in the Arctic," Frank murmured.

"Now, Frank, that's not entirely true," Dovie said, as she slid her arm through Amy's. They strolled down the narrow garden rows, commenting on this plant and that one. The corn was almost knee-high, and the pole beans and other vegetables were well under way.

"I've always wanted a garden," Amy said, and realized how wistful that must have sounded.

"Well, I could certainly use help in mine." Dovie

smiled. "Of course it'd be a little awkward for you this year, but perhaps next."

"I'd like that," Amy said. She'd never known people could be this open and generous.

"Shall we head on over to the health clinic?" Dovie asked.

The walk didn't take more than a few minutes. Amy's hands had grown damp with nerves by the time they arrived. She suspected she'd be the only pregnant woman attending without a husband, and she was right. Three other couples were already inside the clinic waiting. Dovie played hostess, greeting each one and then introducing Amy. Caroline Weston looked to be about six months pregnant, as well, and she and Amy were soon talking comfortably. She was pretty, Amy thought, with her dark brown eyes and soft brown hair. Until now they hadn't been formally introduced, but Amy had chatted with her at the post office when she'd gone to apply for a post-office box.

"Dovie was thrilled you asked her to be your birthing partner," Caroline told her. She sat next to her broad-shouldered rancher husband, Grady Weston.

"I'm the one who's grateful." Amy didn't mind saying so, either. "Being new in town, I was afraid I'd be going through labor alone."

"That would never have happened," Caroline said with confidence. Their eyes met and briefly held. "I wasn't married when I had Maggie," she said softly. "My mother was my labor coach. Jane would have made sure someone supportive was with you."

Caroline was telling Amy far more than the words themselves conveyed. She was saying that at one time she'd walked in the same shoes as Amy. She understood what it meant to stand alone and was offering her encouragement and support. Caroline was married now, and from the tender looks she shared with her husband, it was obvious they were deeply in love.

The class lasted ninety minutes, and the time flew. During the first half hour, everyone spoke for a few moments; Amy, feeling shy, said very little. Then Dr. Jane showed a thirty-minute video of a birth and answered questions. The film had been an eye-opener for Amy. Unlike the others, she hadn't been raised in a ranching community and had never been around farm animals. The baby stirred and kicked as she watched; and Amy felt a surge of pure excitement. The final thirty minutes were spent explaining the breathing techniques used during the early stages of labor.

The key, Amy discovered, was finding a comfortable position. Caroline sat on the carpeted floor and leaned her back against Grady's bent knees and pressed her hands against her stomach. The most comfortable position Amy found was lying flat on her back, knees drawn up. She stared at the ceiling and concentrated on practicing her deep breathing.

Dovie sat by her head and brushed the hair from Amy's brow. Surprisingly Amy discovered that she'd relaxed to the point of nearly drifting off to sleep.

Grady and Caroline offered Dovie and Amy a ride home, but Amy preferred to walk. Dovie did, too.

"Thanks for the offer," Amy said. She was looking forward to the next class—in part because she felt that she and Caroline could easily become friends.

"If I don't see you before, I will at the dance Saturday night," Caroline told Dovie as she climbed inside the car. As if she'd forgotten something important, she poked her head out the open window and gestured to Amy. "You're coming to the big dance, aren't you?"

Amy froze. Dovie had mentioned it earlier, and she'd hoped to avoid the subject altogether. Perhaps—like planting a garden—next year would be better timing.

"Amy?" Dovie urged, apparently waiting for her to respond to Caroline's question.

"I...don't think so," she mumbled, flustered and unsure. She longed to go, but it was impossible. Next year, she thought, when she felt confident again. When she felt like a contributing member of the community. When she was slim again. No man would find her attractive now with her rounding stomach and her ankles swollen by the end of the day. When the time was right—well, she had a man in mind.... It was, admittedly, much too soon to be thinking along those lines, but Wade McMillen was by far the kindest man she'd ever met. Not to mention one of the most attractive!

Caroline waved when Grady pulled the car away from the curb, and Amy waved back.

"So you've decided not to attend the dance," Dovie said, and did nothing to disguise her disappointment.

"I can't," Amy insisted.

"And why's that?"

"A number of reasons."

"The decision is yours, of course," Dovie said, but it was plain the older woman wanted her to reconsider. "However, I think it would do you a world of good to get out and mingle with people your own age. The dance would be the perfect opportunity to do that."

"Next year," she said, but if she'd hoped to appease Dovie, she failed.

"I want you to give me one good reason you feel you should wait."

Obviously Dovie wasn't about to drop the subject with

her usual grace. If anything, she sounded more adamant than she had earlier.

"Oh, Dovie, I wish I could go, but—"

"That does it," Dovie interrupted, cutting her off even before she could complete the thought.

"Does what?"

"You're attending the dance, and I refuse to take no for an answer."

Amy laughed at her friend's stubbornness. "You seem mighty sure of yourself."

"I am." Dovie flashed her a smile that could only be described as smug. "Since I've taken on the role of your fairy godmother, all I need to do now is find the dress and the prince. The dress is simple, and as for the prince—" she giggled with sheer delight "—I know just where to look."

WADE DIDN'T GENERALLY avoid people, especially members of his own congregation, but Dovie Boyd Hennessey had been after him all week to take Amy Thornton to the big dance. He'd given Dovie a flippant response when she first proposed the idea, but the truth of the matter was he *did* like Amy. He admired her courage and determination, her grit. And it didn't hurt any that she was easy on the eyes. When he was with her, Wade forgot he was a pastor and remembered he was a man. He wasn't sure he liked that feeling. He happened to enjoy his life exactly the way it was. Besides, if he was going to ask Amy out, then it would be when he felt ready and not because Dovie Hennessey thought he should. He didn't appreciate being pressured; no one did. So he avoided her.

"I'm not asking you to take Amy as her pastor," she muttered the one time she did manage to catch him—outside the post office. "For the love of heaven, open your eyes, Wade McMillen! Amy's a beautiful young woman."

"My eyes *are* open," Wade said. Far wider than he cared to admit.

Dovie's face relaxed into a knowing grin. "Then the matter's settled."

"Dovie, it isn't a good idea." Wade wasn't about to let her maneuver him into this craziness. At least not without putting up a struggle. "I'm sure once people meet Amy there'll be plenty of men wanting to date her. It wouldn't be fair to saddle her with me so soon after she's arrived."

"That's just an excuse and you know it!"

"I'll tell you what," he said, willing to bend, but only a little. "If no one else has asked her by Friday, then I'll take her myself."

"And insult her like she's some...some castoff. I think not."

There was no satisfying the woman. "Someone else will ask her," he muttered, and left it at that.

Dovie's eyes grew hot enough to cause a nuclear meltdown, but she said nothing more.

Wednesday morning Wade had just ordered the breakfast special at the café in the bowling alley when Sheriff Hennessey slipped into the booth across from him. He righted a coffee mug and motioned to Denise.

"I take it you're avoiding my wife," Frank Hennessey said.

"Can you blame me?" Wade asked.

Frank's tanned face broke into a grin. "I tell you, when Dovie's got a bee in her bonnet, nothing distracts her from getting what she wants." He paused. "I actually feel sorry for you."

Wade had gone over the last conversation with Dovie a dozen times and didn't see how he could do more than he already had. He'd given her his best offer and the woman had insisted he was insulting Amy. This was what made dating hazardous. He saw offering to escort Amy to the dance if no one else invited her as a gesture of kindness. According to Dovie, that wasn't the case. Well, as far as he was concerned, the best thing to do was avoid the dance issue entirely, avoid Dovie, avoid the attraction he felt for Amy—avoid it all.

Denise brought over his breakfast and filled Frank's mug with fresh hot coffee.

"Dovie's talked Amy into attending that dance without a date, so you don't need to worry about her chasing you down any longer."

Wade was relieved and he suspected he had Frank to thank for this unexpected reprieve. "Amy isn't going to have a problem attracting men," Wade said. She was attractive and sweet, and he had no doubt others would soon notice that, too.

A part of Wade, one he didn't want to face, was pleased no one had asked her. He wasn't sure how he'd feel about Amy dating one of the local ranchers, and yet…that was exactly what he wanted, wasn't it?

"Amy's *real* pretty," Frank agreed with him.

Wade didn't appreciate the reminder. "It's just that…"

"Yes?" Frank urged.

Wade longed to explain himself, but he couldn't seem to do it. He didn't understand his own reluctance to invite Amy to the dance, so he said the first logical thing that popped into his head. "I just don't think it's a good idea for a pastor to be romantically linked with an unwed mother. People might get the wrong idea."

Frank held the mug with both hands. He nodded slowly. "I suspect you're right. People are funny about that kind of thing."

Perhaps there was more truth to his words than he realized; Wade no longer knew. Rarely had he felt so confused. It made sense not to complicate his relationship with Amy. For one thing, some folks were sure to make more of a simple date than was warranted. Louise Powell, for instance.

Frank relaxed, leaning back against the red vinyl upholstery, and continued to sip his coffee. "This reminds me of a situation I read about not long ago."

"What situation?" Wade asked.

Frank chuckled. "Dovie's got me reading the Bible these days. She said if I was going to be helping her teach Sunday-school classes, I'd better know what I was talking about."

Wade reached for a slice of bacon, his attention more on his meal than on Frank. "Good idea."

"That's what I thought, too. But there are definite similarities."

Wade was afraid to question too much.

"Between you and that man named Joseph." Frank leaned forward and rested his elbows on the table.

"Joseph?" The bacon had yet to touch his lips.

"You remember him, I'm sure. The one who was engaged to a virgin named Mary. It must have been embarrassing for him, too, don't you think? Here's the woman he's agreed to marry, and she unexpectedly turns up pregnant. Now he loves Mary, but he knows that kid in her belly doesn't belong to him. He also knows that if he continues with the engagement, everyone will believe the worst of him and his bride-to-be."

Wade set the bacon back on his plate.

"Not that I'm suggesting Amy's any virgin, mind you," Frank said.

Wade's appetite had been keen five minutes earlier;

now, what little breakfast he'd managed to swallow sat like a lump of day-old oatmeal in the pit of his stomach. He glared across the table at the sheriff.

"Something wrong, Pastor?" Frank asked. His face broke into a grin. A wide one.

"That was below the belt, Frank."

"How's that?"

"Quoting scripture to a pastor."

"I didn't quote scripture."

Wade pushed his plate aside, appetite gone. "You didn't need to."

"You taking Amy to the dance?"

And Wade had thought that Dovie was less than tactful. He was beginning to understand that husband and wife made one hell of a team. "All right, all right," he said ungraciously, "but I want you to know right now that this is the end of it, understand?"

"Fine. If that's the way you want it."

"I do."

Frank's eyes flew to his. "I do? Isn't that what a groom says when he speaks his vows?" Chuckling, Frank slid from the booth and swaggered out of the café.

Wade was still glaring.

AMY WOULD HAVE BEEN kidding herself if she said she wasn't excited about her date with Wade McMillen.

"Date" might be too strong a word. Two days earlier Wade had phoned and invited her. Amy strongly suspected it was a pity invitation, but at this point pride was no longer as important as it had been. Rather than question what had prompted the invitation, she'd simply accepted.

The instant she got off the phone, Amy had phoned Caroline Weston. While she barely knew her, she felt Caroline was someone she could speak to openly.

Within an hour Amy had received two phone calls. The first one was from Dovie, who promised to bring her the perfect dress. Almost immediately, another call came from Savannah Smith, who was delighted to hear that Wade had asked Amy to the dance. More than delighted. She said it was about time Reverend McMillen realized he was a man, as well as a minister.

The afternoon of the dance, the three women descended on Amy like a swarm of bees.

"Dovie says she's your self-appointed fairy god-mother," Caroline remarked as she walked into the house.

"Just consider us Dovie's assistants." Savannah Smith followed her into the living room, carrying a sleeping baby in an infant seat.

Dovie was the last one to enter the house. She carried a lovely antique white gown in her arms. "Ellie and Jane are coming, too, but they might be a few minutes late."

Amy wasn't sure what to make of all this.

"The way I figure it," Caroline said, studying her watch, "we have approximately two hours."

"Two hours for what?"

Caroline looked at her as though the answer was obvious. "To help our dear pastor realize something he's chosen to ignore for too long."

"Oh…" Amy recalled Savannah's words about Wade. But she didn't understand what, exactly, it had to do with her.

Before Caroline could explain further, the doorbell chimed again.

"Are we too early or too late?" Ellie Patterson asked. Dr. Patterson—Jane—was with her.

"Your timing's perfect," Caroline assured them both.

"What's going on?" Amy asked, still wondering what Caroline and Savannah had meant about Wade. While she appreciated all the attention, it certainly didn't take five women to deliver a dress. Then, suddenly, Amy understood—these women were here to give her a makeover. Apparently she looked worse than she'd realized.

Sagging onto the sofa, she brushed her shoulder-length hair back from her face, using both hands. "I'm hopeless, aren't I?" she said, staring up at the women who crowded her living room.

"Hopeless?" Dovie repeated.

The five women burst out laughing.

"Oh, Amy," Dovie said gently, "it's just the opposite." She sat down next to her and reached for Amy's hand, holding it between both of her own. "We're not here to make you beautiful. You already are."

"Then why…?"

Caroline and Savannah exchanged glances as if to decide who would say it.

"We're here to bring Wade McMillen to his knees," Caroline said.

"But he's been wonderful to me!"

"He'll be more than wonderful once we get finished with you," Ellie insisted.

The other women appeared to be in full agreement.

"What do you think of this hairstyle?" Savannah flipped open a magazine for Amy to inspect. The picture revealed an advertisement for cosmetics with a pencil-thin model wearing a black evening gown There was a slit in the dress that stretched all the way up her thigh and her hair was a mussed flock of red curls. She clutched a strand of diamonds to her nonexistent breasts and threw back her head in laughter.

Not in two lifetimes would Amy resemble this model.

"Do you like the hair?" Savannah pressed.

"The flat stomach appeals to me a whole lot more."

"In time," Savannah promised.

If Laura's mother was an example, then Amy had hope. The infant, asleep in the portable carrier, wasn't more than three or four months old, and Savannah was as trim as a teenager. Amy had begun to wonder if she'd ever get her shape back.

Every day she discovered that more clothes no longer fit. She wore her jeans with the zipper open and a large sweatshirt pulled over them. Even the elastic bands around her two skirts had been stretched beyond recognition.

"I brought a few maternity clothes I thought you might need," Savannah whispered. "I figured we're about the same size. Unfortunately Caroline's too tall to wear anything of mine. Use them if you want and pass them on when you're through."

Then the transformation began. While Savannah brushed her hair, Ellie did Amy's nails and Caroline applied her makeup. When she'd finished, she started on her own.

Amy felt her eyes smart with tears and quickly blinked them away. "Why would you all do something so kind for a stranger?" she asked.

"A stranger?" Ellie squeezed Amy's hand. "You aren't a stranger."

"But I could rob everyone blind," she said, tossing out her arms. "I could run away in that dress."

"But you won't," Dovie said confidently.

"What makes you so sure?"

Dovie paused and gave a casual shrug. "After all these years, I think I've become a good judge of people. You, Amy, are one of the special ones."

"Don't you even think about crying," Caroline said, waving a mascara wand in her right hand. "You'll ruin your eye makeup."

Amy blinked furiously and the six of them broke into peals of laughter.

"Actually," Jane said, flopping down on the sofa, "let's be honest here and admit the truth. We like you, Amy. You haven't lived here a month, and already you're one of us."

Amy smiled, because that was the way she felt, too.

"Now let's be even more honest," Jane said. "We're here on account of Wade."

The others were quick to agree.

"Wade?" Amy repeated.

"Wade," they said in unison.

"I'm afraid," Dovie said kindly, "that our dear pastor needs to be brought down a peg or two, and we've decided you're the one to do it."

"What has he done?"

"He's gotten…" Jane searched for the right word.

"Smug," Ellie supplied. "Set in his ways and too damned sure he's got everything in his life all figured out. He needs a bit of shaking up."

The others nodded. "He's a little too arrogant," Savannah said.

"About the church?" That didn't sound anything like the Wade Amy had come to know.

"No, not with the church," Savannah replied, looking thoughtful.

"We're talking about…"

None of her friends seemed to want to say the word. They glanced at one another.

"Romance?" Amy finally suggested.

"Exactly," Dovie said, rubbing her palms together. "He's gotten rather…stodgy when it comes to matters of the heart. He's a little too sure he doesn't need love and marriage—that they don't fit with being a pastor."

"And we felt it was time someone opened his eyes."

"You think I'm the one to do that?" Amy found the suggestion highly amusing.

"You're not taking us seriously, are you?" Caroline asked.

"How can I?" Amy giggled. "Have any of you happened to notice I'm pregnant?"

"All the better," Ellie muttered. "Wade McMillen is about to get a crash course."

"You ready, girls?" Savannah asked, and pulled a hair dryer from deep inside the diaper bag.

"Ready," came a chorus of replies.

For the next while Savannah worked endlessly getting Amy's thick hair to curl like the redheaded model's in the magazine. Amy wasn't allowed to look in a mirror. While Savannah worked on her, Caroline painted her own nails and Ellie stood in front of the living-room mirror and tested a new brand of eyeliner.

"I don't think Frank ever dreamed his house would turn into a women's dressing room," Dovie teased.

They laughed again. When Laura awoke and wailed for her mother, Amy was sure the infant hadn't been asleep more than a few minutes. She was astonished to realize it had been two hours.

"My goodness, where did the afternoon go?"

"Are you ready to take a look in the mirror?" Jane asked.

Amy considered the question and nodded. The others instructed her to close her eyes, then the six of them trooped into the bedroom. Jane guided Amy to a spot in front of the full-length mirror.

"Okay, open your eyes."

The first thing Amy saw was the five women gathered around her, all smiling gleefully. Her own reflection stunned her. The transformation was complete. She'd never looked more glamorous, more lovely. Amy felt like Cinderella.

"What do you think?" Caroline asked.

"I…don't know what to say."

"You're gonna knock him for a loop," Jane said confidently.

"And the best part is," Ellie said, standing next to her sister-in-law, "we're all going to be there to see it happen."

WADE MCMILLEN muttered under his breath as he slipped the string tie with the turquoise clasp over his head. He adjusted it and headed for the front door.

He wasn't sure how he'd gotten roped into this date. This would be the first time he'd taken anyone to the big dance. He wasn't sure it was a precedent he wanted to set. Not only that, he'd been finagled into the date and it didn't sit well with him.

Amy was a sweet kid. *But that's exactly what she is,* he reminded himself. *A kid.* Twenty-five was far too young for a man of thirty-three. If he was going to become romantically involved, then it would be with… Unfortunately no one came to mind.

He blamed Frank for this whole thing, right along with Dovie. The two people he'd helped out when they'd reached an impasse several months back. And this was the thanks he got.

Wade closed his eyes and groaned. Amy was young and pretty. Young enough and pretty enough to set Louise Powell's tongue wagging, that was for sure. Well, let the troublemaker talk all she wanted. She would, anyway, and anything he said in his own defense was sure to be misconstrued.

So he'd take Amy to the Grange hall tonight, and he'd dance with her, too, if that was what she wanted. But he fully intended to introduce her around. Charlie Engler might be interested. Steve Ellis, too. Both owned smaller spreads seventy or eighty miles outside Promise. They usually drove into town on Friday afternoons and split their time between the feed store and drinking beer at Billy D's. Lyle Whitehouse was often with them, but Wade wanted to steer Amy away from him. Lyle had a temper and tended to enjoy his liquor a little too much.

What Charlie and Steve needed, Wade figured, was a stabilizing influence. A wife and ready-made family would go a long way toward setting either man on the right path.

That decided, Wade reached for his Stetson, then locked the front door. He whistled as he drove toward Frank's old house. He hadn't thought to get Amy a corsage and stopped at the local Winn-Dixie on his way. Nothing fancy. He couldn't see investing a lot of money in a bunch of dyed blue carnations that were sure to get squashed when she danced. Besides *he* wouldn't be the one to smell their fragrance. Charlie would. Maybe Steve.

He parked his Blazer at the curb and hopped out. His smile was already in place when he rang the doorbell. Knowing Dovie had helped Amy find a decent dress, he wanted to be sure he complimented her on how pretty she looked.

He pressed the doorbell with one hand and held the flower in the other.

An inordinate amount of time passed—at least two minutes—and Wade pressed the bell again. The door opened just then and a fashion model stood before him. His mouth must have dropped open; all he could do was stare. This had to be a joke and if so he wasn't amused.

"I'm here for Amy," he said, wondering who was behind this scheme.

"Wade, it's me," she said, and laughed softly.

Chapter Four

Nell Bishop felt like an entertainment director aboard a cruise ship. Her dude ranch was in full operation now, and the second group of cowboy wanna-bes had thought it would be great fun to end their adventure by attending the dance put on by the local Cattlemen's Association.

There were four men and two women, all gussied up in their finest Western gear. She'd driven them to the festivities in the used minivan she'd bought at the first of the month. So far, her plan to turn Twin Canyons into a dude ranch, complete with a trail drive and sleeping under the stars, had been an unqualified success.

Of course Nell had gotten plenty of help along the way. Her mother-in-law, Ruth, and her children, Jeremy and Emma, had been indispensable; so were the two hands she'd hired.

The crazy part was that after spending a year and a half planning and developing her idea, she was ready to abandon everything—for love. Travis Grant was to blame for this sudden change of heart.

Nell remained on the edge of the dance floor, watching old Pete Hadley, who stood on the stage, a fiddle tucked under his chin, accompanying a country-and-western band.

Couples formed uniform rows and performed the latest in line dances.

Men and women alike slid across the polished wood floor, looking like a scene out of a 1930's Hollywood musical, and all Nell could think about was how much she missed Travis. The engagement ring on her finger was testimony of his love. Although they spoke daily by phone, it wasn't enough. They were eager to marry, eager to start their lives together.

Unfortunately planning a time for their wedding wasn't a simple matter. Nell had obligations, and so did he. Because of the dude ranch, she was forced to stay in Texas. A summer in New York would have been a fabulous cultural experience for Jeremy and Emma, but it wasn't possible. Not this year.

Nor could Travis just pack his bags and move to Texas. Not yet. Like her, he had commitments. Speaking engagements, an author tour, followed by a research trip that had been booked for more than a year. Being apart like this wasn't what he wanted, either, but it couldn't be helped.

Three months, he'd told her, and then they'd be together for the rest of their lives. It hadn't sounded so bad when he first outlined his schedule. The weeks would fly by, he'd said, and they had. It was almost July now, and soon August would arrive and before she knew it, September. On the first Saturday of September Travis and Nell would become husband and wife.

"Nell." Caroline Weston stopped in front of the punch bowl beside Nell. "My goodness, I can't remember the last time I saw you. You look fantastic. How are you?"

"Wonderful," Nell told her friend, which was the truth. But if anyone looked fantastic, it was Caroline. Her pregnancy was obvious now and she literally glowed with an inner contentment. "You must be so happy." Nell was pleased that Caroline had found her cowboy at last. Grady Weston might be stubborn and quick-tempered, but he was a man who would love and honor his wife.

Caroline's face flushed with pleasure as she rested her hands on her stomach. "I've never felt better."

Grady joined his wife. He stood behind Caroline and caressed her shoulders. "Good to see you, Nell. How's the dude ranch going?"

"It's keeping me busy," she said. Her gaze wandered to the dance floor, and she was gratified to see that her guests were enjoying themselves. Two couples and two male business executives made up her current group. They were a good mix; everyone had gotten along well. Nell didn't expect that to be the case with every two-week session and considered herself fortunate.

"My feet need a rest," Caroline announced, and Grady led his wife to a row of chairs that lined one wall. A number of spectators sat there, visiting with one another.

Nell watched as Grady and Caroline joined them. Once she was comfortable, Grady brought his wife something cool to drink. Nell smiled absently and tapped her foot to the music. A year earlier, Grady had unexpectedly phoned and invited her to this very dance. She'd gotten two invitations, in fact—one from Glen Patterson, as well—and now, a brief twelve months later, both Grady and Glen were married.

The ache of loneliness inside Nell increased. Travis Grant was a city slicker, her first guest on the dude ranch, and she'd fallen head over heels in love with him. And he with her. Both had been married before. Nell was a widow, and Travis was divorced. Neither had any intention of falling in love again. But they'd been thrown together working to solve the mystery that surrounded Bitter End, the ghost town situated outside Promise. Eagerly on Travis's part, reluctantly on hers. But after research and much conjecture, they *had* solved it. In the process they'd fallen in love.

At first a lasting relationship between them had seemed impossible. Travis had returned to New York, and she'd resumed the business of her life, starting a new venture and raising her two children. But she'd been miserable. Travis, too. It wasn't long—less than two weeks—before they both realized they belonged together. They'd intended to get married right away. So much for best-laid plans. September had never seemed as far away as it did right that minute.

The music slowed and couples moved into each other's arms. Nell missed Travis so much that watching the dancers was almost painful. She was about to turn away when someone tapped her shoulder.

"I believe this dance is mine."

She instantly recognized the rich resonant voice. *Travis.* But that wasn't possible. He was touring on the East Coast and not due back in New York until Sunday. Not due in Texas until right before their wedding.

Nell whirled around, convinced her heart was playing tricks on her. "Travis?" Her shocked afraid-to-believe gaze met his. After a second of stunned wonder, she hurled herself into his arms.

Travis clasped Nell around the waist and, in his joy, half lifted her from the ground. Without caring about an audience, she spread kisses all over his face. "Travis, oh, Travis."

She didn't know how he happened to arrive in Texas for this dance or how long he could stay. None of that was important just then. Being in his arms was.

"Let's dance," he whispered, and reached for her hand.

Numb with happiness, she blindly followed him onto the floor.

Dancing was little more than a convenient excuse to continue holding each other. Nell closed her eyes as she moved into his embrace, listening to the slow mellow music. With her arms around his neck and her face against his shoulder, she clung to him and he to her. All too soon the dance ended, long before Nell was ready, and from the reluctant way he released her, she knew Travis wasn't ready, either. With no other choice they broke apart and applauded politely.

"How... When?" she asked as they walked off the dance floor. In her shock, she had trouble getting the words out.

Travis took her hand and led her to a quiet corner, away from the festivities. They sat facing each other, so close their knees touched.

"I phoned late yesterday afternoon," he began. "You weren't there. I was feeling miserable without you and exhausted from the tour. I was scheduled to fly back to New York last night."

Nell knew that much already.

"All at once I realized I didn't give a tinker's damn if I ever saw the New York skyline again. Everything that's important to me is right here in Promise."

"Why didn't you let me know..?"

He grinned and touched her cheek as if he couldn't believe, even now, that they were together. "Ruth answered the phone and we talked. She told me you'd been working too hard."

"I haven't, it's just that— Oh, Travis, it's so wonderful to see you." If they'd been anyplace other than a crowded dance with half the town looking on, she would've kissed him senseless. She had so much to tell him, so much she wanted to ask in the little time they had before he left again. His promotional tour might be over, but he was scheduled to leave almost immediately on a research trip deep in the interior of Mexico.

Travis touched her face and his eyes brightened with intensity. ''I'm not taking that trip.''

''But Travis, you've been planning it for so long.''

''I'll go someday, but when I do it'll be with you. I didn't know it was possible to feel this strongly about someone. As far as I'm concerned, the entire book tour was a waste. My publicist said that next time the publisher plans anything like this, they'll gladly pay to have you fly with me. I wasn't worth a damn. Look what you've done to me, Nell.''

She smiled. ''How long can you stay?'' she asked.

Travis glanced at his watch and Nell realized he'd probably need to be back on the road by morning.

''Does the next forty years suit you?''

''What?'' His response completely unsettled her.

''I want us to get married.''

''Now?''

''As soon as we can set it up with Wade,'' he said. ''We'll leave on our honeymoon right away. Somewhere wonderful, anywhere, I don't care as long as we're together.''

''But I can't go now.'' Nell's heart sank. ''I can't leave the ranch.'' Although her guests were due to depart the next morning, a fresh batch was scheduled to arrive first thing Monday.

''It's all been arranged,'' Travis insisted.

''Arranged? What do you mean?''

''Actually this was all Ruth's idea. She asked me to remind you of a surprise birthday party you threw for her last year. Well, this little surprise is her doing.'' Travis grinned. "Ruth's got your bags packed and says she refuses to listen to any excuses."

"What about—"

"It's covered, sweetheart. Ruth got two of her retired friends to come in and ride roughshod over the next bunch of greenhorns. Everything's under control, so don't worry."

"But—"

"We're getting married, Nell, no ifs, ands or buts!"

"Yes, oh, Travis, yes." Nell was overcome with gratitude—and with joy—that he was here and she was in his arms...and they were getting married!

"I knew you'd agree once you heard my plan."

Smiling through her tears, Nell hugged the greenhorn who'd captured her heart. Ruth had said that one day she'd give her a surprise as big as the birthday party Nell had thrown for her. Nell had never dreamed it would be something this wonderful.

"I'm crazy about you," Travis whispered.

Wonderful, indeed.

AFTER ACTING like an idiot at Amy's front door, Wade had quickly recovered his composure by making some ridiculous comment about the sunlight blinding his eyes.

He'd been blinded all right, but it wasn't by the sun. Just then he suspected it had been his own stupidity that had done him in.

The Lord had quite a sense of humor, Wade reflected. He considered what happened a sort of a divine-induced attitude adjustment. From the way he'd behaved, anyone might have thought that taking Amy to this dance was a burden. An unpleasant chore. He'd done everything but hide in an effort to avoid it. In reality, he was so calf-eyed over her it was all he could do to keep the drool off his chin. What he'd needed was a good swift kick in the rear. And Amy had provided it.

The minute they'd arrived, Amy had received more attention than a Smithsonian exhibit. Single ranchers had immediately flocked around her; two hours later, they still did. Wade had never seen anything like it.

No sooner had they stepped into the hall than Steve Ellis had asked for a dance. The guy had his nerve! Wade hadn't seen any of the other men stopping and requesting a dance from someone else's date. What really stuck in his craw was that the evening was half over and he had yet to dance with Amy.

He couldn't get close enough to ask.

Okay, okay, so this was probably what he deserved. He was the first to admit his attitude had been all wrong. He'd made a mistake in not owning up to the way he felt about her. A big mistake—but it seemed he wasn't going to get the opportunity to undo it.

This sudden interest was due to more than simply the fact that Amy was a beautiful woman. Anyone looking at her could see that. On the drive to the dance he'd struggled to keep his eyes on the road and not on her. So, okay, he was attracted to her. He liked her, too. Really liked her, and had from the first.

But he'd been afraid of what people would say if he pursued a relationship with her. A romance. Fear had dominated his actions.

Sheriff Hennessey had tried to talk sense into him. Unfortunately Wade's stubborn pride had prevented him from hearing the message. He resented being manipulated, and he'd focused on that, instead of his feelings for Amy.

From this point forward he refused to allow what others thought to dictate his decisions. He wanted to get to know Amy better. If she wasn't ready to date, then he'd start by being her friend. She was a generous person and he hoped she'd be willing to give him a second chance. That was, if he could manage to break through the throng of men vying for her attention.

At social events such as this, Wade made a point of dancing with the older single women, widows and the like. Women his mother's and grandmother's ages. Tonight, however, he couldn't make himself do it. The only person he wanted to hold in his arms was Amy Thornton—his date. So far, unfortunately, he'd only seen her from a distance.

"Are you enjoying yourself?" Dovie sneaked in the question as she danced past him on Frank's arm. The smile in her eyes told Wade she was well aware of how miserable he was.

Dovie Boyd Hennessey had a mean streak in her, he thought grimly. One that cut to the bone.

"Pretty as a picture, isn't she?" Frank asked as they glided past him a second time.

Wade didn't need to ask who they meant, either. But then he'd made it fairly obvious. He hadn't been able to take his eyes off Amy all night. He was about to turn away and bury his sorrows in a plate from the buffet when the dance ended. Whether by luck or design, Amy stood next to him. She slid her arm through his and gave a deep sigh.

"I've got to sit down for a bit," she said to him. "My feet are killing me."

Here she was, the woman he'd been patiently waiting to dance with all night, and for the life of him, Wade couldn't think of a sensible thing to say.

She gazed up at him as though she'd been anticipating this moment the entire evening. "I hope you don't mind."

"No, ah…sure." His tongue refused to cooperate and work properly. He glanced over his shoulder and saw

Grady and Caroline seated close by. Caroline's feet rested in his lap and Grady was rubbing her nylon-covered toes. The scene was intimate, the husbandly gesture loving and thoughtful. The ache inside Wade caught him unawares. In the last year a number of his friends had married, and while he was happy for them, he didn't feel the need for a wife and family himself. He'd always seen his life as complete, viewed his pastoral duties as too demanding for marriage. His satisfaction came from his work, and it was enough—or so he believed. In that moment, however—and other moments like it—he felt keenly alone.

"We can sit here," he said, finally clearing his head. He escorted Amy to an empty section of seats and sat down next to her.

"Thank you," she whispered, and sent him a warm smile.

Wade nearly drowned in her beautiful eyes. He saw her slip out of her shoes and wiggle her toes a couple of times. Then, feeling remiss, he asked, "Would you like something to drink?"

She nodded, her eyes grateful. "That would be wonderful, but nothing alcoholic."

Wade wanted to kick himself, convinced that the minute he left someone would take his seat. He'd been waiting for an opportunity like this and now he was going to lose it.

Sure enough, as soon as he reached the punch bowl, Lyle Whitehouse was standing beside her, leaning against a chair. He looked like he was about to sit down when he suddenly stared over at Wade. Then he nodded and after a couple of seconds walked away.

Wade made it back in record time, nearly stumbling over his own feet in his effort to get to her before some other rancher did.

"Here you go," he said, handing her the plastic cup. "Uh, how do you like the dance so far?" he asked, trying to make small talk.

"I'm having a wonderful time."

No doubt, Wade mused darkly, seeing as she'd danced every dance, and each one had been with a different partner. *Not* including him. But when Pete Hadley and the band started a favorite song of Wade's from the movie *Dirty Dancing,* "She's like the Wind," it was impossible to hold still.

"I know your shoes are off," he said, "but would you care to take a spin?"

Wade wasn't sure what he expected, but not such a quick agreement. "I'd like that."

She slipped her feet back into her shoes and he extended a hand to help her up. They walked onto the dance floor and he took her in his arms. She was tiny, eight or nine inches shorter than he was, which put the top of her head level with his shoulder. Yet they fit together nicely.

Wade wasn't exactly light on his feet, but he could manage a simple slow dance. Amy followed his lead as though they'd been partners for years. He hummed along with the song and was surprised when her soft voice joined his, harmonizing. They smiled at each other, and he gathered her closer.

That was when it happened. The baby kicked. Wade's eyes widened at the strength of the movement. "I didn't realize I'd be able to feel the baby," he said with awe. "That's really something."

"I think she likes the music."

"She?"

"Or he, but since I don't know, I decided to call the baby Sarah."

"And what if she's a he? Do you have a boy's name picked out?"

"Joseph."

That was appropriate, he thought, remembering what Frank had reminded him of the biblical story of Joseph and Mary. Appropriate and a little uncanny.

"A good solid name," he murmured, trying not to let his reaction show.

The song ended far too soon to suit him. He hated to ask Amy to dance again, knowing how worn-out she was, but he couldn't resist. "One more dance?"

She looked up and nodded. He might have been mistaken, but she seemed pleased that he'd asked.

AMY KNEW HOW CINDERELLA must have felt the night of the ball when she first danced with her prince, because that was exactly how she felt just then. All evening she'd waited for Wade to ask her; when it seemed he never would, she gave up. Then the minute she sat down he'd asked.

This was quite possibly the most wonderful night of her life, she mused as Wade held her close. The baby had decided to take up marching and was halfway to Pretoria when she did a swift about-face and kicked Wade. To Amy's delight, he'd been fascinated.

Her fairy godmother, in the guise of Dovie Hennessey, caught sight of her on the dance floor with Wade and winked. Amy winked back and managed to stifle a laugh.

Never in all her life had Amy been this popular with men. From the moment she arrived, she'd been bombarded with requests to dance. When she was first approached, she'd hoped Wade would explain to the others that she was his date. He hadn't done that. Amy knew he hadn't been excited about taking her to the dance and so, rather than burden him with her company, she'd accepted. But truth be known, Wade McMillen was the man she wanted to dance with, more than anyone.

He'd stood by most of the evening, watching her with everyone else, and that had been a bitter disappointment. Only she wasn't disappointed now.

Once they were on the dance floor, Wade didn't seem eager to leave. Amy didn't want to, either. If she closed her eyes, she could pretend that the man who held her was in love with her and wanted this baby. It was a silly fantasy, born of her need to create a secure happy world for her child.

She'd loved Alex with all her heart, but she'd been foolishly blind to his selfishness. For most of her life she'd been more parent than child to her own mother. It had come as no surprise that her mother cut herself off from her just at the time she'd needed her most. Disappointed though she was, Amy could handle the rejection because it was such a familiar experience. Even an expected one.

But Alex had lied to her and hurt her. Deeply. That was one reason this attraction to Wade had surprised her. Now that she was in his arms, even if it was on a dance floor, she couldn't make herself think of him as her pastor. He was a man. Vital, real and handsome.

The baby kicked again, harder this time, and Amy heard Wade chuckle.

"She's got good taste in music," he whispered close to her ear.

"Her mommy's fond of Roy Orbison, too."

"Would you mind if I..." Wade paused as though he wasn't sure he should proceed.

"You'd like to feel the baby?" she asked, tilting her head up just enough to look into his eyes.

"If you don't mind."

"I don't." She took his hand and pressed his palm against her stomach, holding it there. Sarah cooperated beautifully and Amy watched as his face took on a look of reverence and surprise.

"My goodness," he whispered. "That really is something," he said again.

"You should feel her from my end," Amy teased.

His expressive eyes brightened and he broke into a full smile.

"What took you so long?" she asked, feeling content. "The evening was half over before you even asked me to dance."

"I'm a fool. But—" he grinned sheepishly "—I'm a fast learner."

"Good."

The rest of the evening passed far too quickly for Amy. She could have danced with him all night, especially those slow, languid dances. What pleased her the most, perhaps, was how comfortable she felt with Wade. For a few hours it was as though all the worries and problems she'd carried alone all this time had been lifted from her shoulders.

Reality would return soon enough, but for now it was easy to pretend, easy to push her troubles aside and concentrate, instead, on the handsome prince smiling down on her.

Then it was midnight and time to head home. Following the dance, Wade and Amy were invited to a party at Glen and Ellie's place. Amy would have liked to go, but realized Wade had church services early the next morning. It didn't seem fair to keep him up half the night simply because she was in a party mood.

They sang along with the radio on the ride back into Promise. The drive out had been spent in silence, and while they'd done little real talking that evening, Amy felt they'd reached a tacit understanding. She felt they'd achieved an appreciation and acceptance of each other that had been missing previously.

Wade parked under the large weeping willow in front of the house. Moonlight filtered through the branches and cast a silvery glow about them.

Amy reflected on her unexpectedly wonderful evening. Her magical evening with Wade McMillen. Dancing with him, being held by him, was everything she'd known it would be. And she knew with certainty that this was the kind of man she wanted as a father to her child, the kind of man she wanted one day to marry. She'd given up thinking men like him still existed.

"I can't thank you enough," she said, leaning back against the seat and closing her eyes. "Oh, Wade, I had such a lovely time."

"I enjoyed myself, too."

She sighed, her heart full of joy and, yes, gratitude.

"The Fourth of July will be here before we know it," he said.

Amy had heard about the annual Willie Nelson Fourth of July picnic. The community faithfully invited Willy every year, but he'd never managed to come—and then he'd shocked everyone by showing up last spring for the annual rodeo and chili cook-off.

"Do you have any plans?" Wade asked.

"For the Fourth? None." Her hopes soared; surely he'd mentioned the holiday as a preamble to inviting her to join him. It was crazy to think this way, for a lot of reasons. She suspected he was reluctant to become romantically involved, because of his work. But she couldn't keep her heart from hoping... And for her, the timing was difficult, to say the least.

"I understand the community has a big picnic every year in the park," she added, encouraging him to continue.

"I've never been."

"You haven't?" Amy couldn't imagine what had kept him away.

"My family has a big get-together every year. It's quite a shindig."

Amy envied him his family.

"I was just thinking," he said, "that maybe you'd like to come this year."

"With you?"

"Unless, of course, you'd rather attend the community festivities."

Amy was afraid to reveal how eager she was to go with him. "No, I'd rather... I—thank you." She smiled tentatively. "I'd enjoy meeting your family." The baby stirred and Amy bit her lip. In retrospect, perhaps now wouldn't be the best time to meet Wade's parents. She could only imagine what they'd think when their preacher son arrived with a pregnant woman. That gave new meaning to the words "family outing."

As a child Amy used to wonder what it would be like to be part of a traditional family. A real family, where people cared about each other, where they shared things and celebrated together. A mother and father, brother and sister, grandparents. She'd experienced none of that, and she longed for it.

"Are you sure you want me to meet your parents...like this?" she felt obliged to ask.

"I wouldn't have asked you otherwise," Wade told her with a sincerity that couldn't be questioned.

They sat side by side, talking quietly for another five minutes before Amy yawned. She didn't want this incredible evening ever to end, but her eyes were closing despite her resolve.

"Let's get you inside," Wade suggested. He had his car door open before she could protest.

Reluctantly Amy straightened and let him help her out of the car. At the beginning of the night she'd felt young and full of energy. Six hours later, her feet hurt, her legs were weak and shaky, and she was more exhausted than she could remember being in her entire life. Exhausted...but happy.

Wade placed his arm around her as they walked up the sidewalk toward the small house. Until they reached the front porch, Amy hadn't given the matter of a good-night kiss a single thought. Now she turned to Wade, wondering what he'd do. He seemed as uncertain as she was.

"Well," he said, taking a step back. "I had a great time."

So he'd decided against it. That was fine; she understood. Perhaps next time, even if she felt a little disappointed now.

"Thank you for taking me to the dance," Amy said formally, opening her handbag to search for the key.

"Amy?"

She glanced up, and when she did, she realized that he intended to kiss her. And she intended to let him.

Chapter Five

Wade had officiated at a few hurried weddings, but none in which the bride had less than forty-eight hours to prepare. The bride and the entire community. The first Wade had heard of Nell and Travis's wedding was Sunday, after services. Travis announced they'd be applying for the license Monday morning and would greatly appreciate it if Wade could marry them that same evening.

Sure enough, Monday evening the couple stood before him, surrounded by family and friends. In his years as a minister, he'd performed dozens of marriages. Most engaged couples attended several weeks of counseling first. Generally he hesitated to marry people who were in too much of a rush. Nell and Travis hadn't taken his counseling sessions, but he'd talked extensively with them both when they became engaged. They showed all the signs of making their marriage strong and lasting. They were committed to each other and to their relationship. While deeply in love, neither was ruled by passion. Both were mature adults who were accepting and encouraging of each other.

Outwardly their differences seemed overwhelming. Travis lived in New York City and Nell single-handedly managed a cattle ranch near Promise. Travis was a well-known author and Nell a struggling businesswoman. But

Wade soon realized their differences were superficial; what they had in common was far more important. They shared not only a deep love but a goal, a vision for the future. A vision that had to do with creating a supportive and loving home for each other and for Nell's family. Wade didn't have one qualm about this rushed wedding.

Nell might have had only forty-eight hours to prepare for her wedding, but the church was as lovely as he'd ever seen it. The sanctuary had been decorated with roses and candles whose flickering light cast an enchanted glow over those who'd gathered to share the moment with Travis and Nell. Savannah Smith had supplied armloads of red roses, arranging them in glittering crystal vases. Wade couldn't recall seeing any roses lovelier than the ones from Savannah's lush garden, certainly none with a more glorious scent.

Wade smiled at the couple. Given that the wedding was being held with little prior notice, no invitations had been mailed. But word had been passed on the street. It surprised Wade that so many people had come tonight to share in Nell's joy. Then again, it didn't. The folks in Promise admired Nell, so they wanted to stand with her as she pledged her heart to Travis. Grateful for the role he'd played in resolving the mystery of Bitter End, the town had accepted Travis as one of their own. People were happy for the couple and looked to show their support.

After a few introductory words Wade opened his Bible. When he'd finished, he glanced up, prepared to ask Nell and Travis to repeat their vows. As he did, he noticed Amy sitting next to Dovie and Frank.

He'd seen her briefly following the Sunday service, but she'd slipped away before he was able to seek her out. The night of the dance had been a revelation to him; he'd finally acknowledged how he felt about her. Finally acknowledged that he felt an attraction to Amy—that he wanted to pursue a relationship with her, even if it threw his whole life into chaos. Which it would.

When they danced, he'd felt her baby move against him and an unfamiliar emotion had stirred deep inside him. Later, he'd placed his palm over her extended stomach and it was as though her child had leaped to greet him. Then, he'd brought her home and kissed her good-night. The moment had been fleeting, but her kiss had stayed with him for hours afterward. Was with him still. In the two days since, he'd thought of little except Amy and her child. He wondered if she'd been thinking of him, too. And hoped she had. Even now, in the middle of a wedding, it was all he could do not to stare at her.

He hadn't expected Amy to be here tonight, but he was glad she'd come—if for no other reason than he could see her again.

"Travis, do you take…" Wade continued speaking, the words as much a part of him as the scripture passage he routinely read in the marriage ceremony. Yet, again and again, his attention wandered back to Amy, as if drawn to her by an invisible force.

After the ceremony the congregation applauded loudly. Travis kissed Nell, and when they broke apart, Nell's face was flushed with happiness. She hugged her children as Ruth, her mother-in-law, dabbed at her eyes with a handkerchief.

Beaming, Travis pumped Wade's hand, then hugged Jeremy and Emma, Nell's son and daughter. Wade laughed outright when Travis kissed a flustered Ruth on the cheek.

Dovie had baked a wedding cake and that, along with coffee, was being served in the church hall immediately afterward.

Wade waited until the church was empty, blew out the

candles and followed the crowd to the reception. He found himself standing next to Amy, who was eating a thin slice of cake.

"That was a beautiful ceremony," she said.

"Weddings and baptisms are my specialties."

She patted her stomach. "Sarah's pleased to hear that."

"Has she been marching around much today?"

"Like a drum majorette."

Wade chuckled. He finished his cake and set the paper plate aside. "I wanted you to know how much I enjoyed the dance on Saturday night."

"I did, too." Her cheeks went pink. "I'm looking forward to spending the Fourth of July with you and your family."

There was no further time to talk; Travis approached them, thanking Wade jubilantly. He also thanked Amy for coming to share in their happiness.

Forty minutes after the ceremony Nell and Travis were gone and the hall had emptied. Dovie and a couple of other women from the church had stayed behind to clean up. Amy was with them, ready to pitch in and do what she could.

Wade made his way back to the sanctuary to turn out the lights and lock up the church for the night. The peaceful silence was a distinct contrast to the noise and merry-making of the reception. He slipped into a pew; he liked to check in with the "Boss" now and then when something was weighing on his mind.

Wade leaned forward, bracing his elbows on his knees. "Okay, okay, so I'll admit it, I'm attracted to her. There, I said it, are you happy? If you were sending me a wake-up call, then I received it loud and clear. I like her—and I liked kissing her. You've got my attention." He raised his head. "Now what?"

Why a scene from the church dinner nearly a year ago would flash into his mind just then, Wade couldn't say. It was one of the biggest social functions held by the church, and he remembered how difficult it'd been to find a place to sit. His friends were all busy with their wives or lady friends. It was one of the only times Wade could remember feeling alone. Shortly afterward he'd given some thought to seeking a romantic relationship. He'd gone so far as to make up a list. He'd completely forgotten that or where he'd placed it.

His Bible.

He reached for the leather-bound volume at his side and found the tattered slip of paper tucked under the fly leaf. What he read was:

1. A woman who loves God as much as she does me.
2. A woman as interested in a family as I am.
3. Long legs.

He laughed out loud at the last request. His smile slowly faded and it seemed as if the voice in his heart wasn't as still or as small as it had been in the past.

"Amy?" he said aloud. God had sent Amy for him?

Sighing deeply, Wade leaned back against the wooden pew. An argument rose fast and furious within him, then died just as quickly. The strength of the attraction he felt for her had overwhelmed him the night of the dance. Afterward, too.

Questions crowded his heart. "I don't mean to complain, Lord, but are you sure you sent me the right woman?"

Silence.

"All right, all right, I get the message. I asked. You sent. I shouldn't complain. It's not that I object to Amy, mind you," he whispered, "it's just that…" What? "Just that…" he began again, and realized he was afraid. Not of falling in love. He was ready for that; he'd come to terms with the prospect of upheaval in his life—had even begun to look forward to it. But he was afraid of what he didn't know. He didn't want to demand answers or pry into her life, but it wasn't as if he could ignore the pregnancy, either.

He was afraid of making an emotional commitment to her and her baby, and then watching her walk out on him. Afraid of loving her and risking his heart.

Amy Thornton had come into his life, looking for a few miracles. What he hadn't understood at the time was that she might accomplish a few miracles of her own.

GRADY WESTON'S long hard day had been spent driving his herd of stubborn cattle from one range to another. The sun beat down on him with an intensity that was a prelude of what would come later in the summer.

He felt good. About life. About love. About his family. In about three months he and Caroline would be parents for the second time. Maggie was his daughter in every way that mattered. The father's name had been left blank on the birth certificate, so he'd been able to adopt her shortly after he married Caroline. But this pregnancy would be the first time he'd experienced all the emotion and joy that came before the actual birth.

Boy or girl, as far as Grady was concerned he'd be happy with either. Even without knowing, he loved this child with a fierceness that was equaled only by his love for Maggie.

He recalled the night his sister had given birth to Laura Rose. Laredo had been hopeless, barely able to function. Grady had found his brother-in-law's actions somewhat amusing, but as Caroline's time drew near, Grady suspected he wouldn't be much better. Already he worried about her. He wished he could talk her into quitting her job at the post office early, but she was determined to work until the last minute. Whether or not she'd return to work after the baby was born was entirely up to her. She'd mentioned she might take a few years off and go back once their youngest had reached school age. He hoped she would; for her own sake more than his.

Grady looked up and was surprised to see someone approach. He strained his eyes, not recognizing the rider until he came closer. It was Wade McMillen. He couldn't imagine what the reverend might want, unless it was to announce some kind of trouble. Studying the rider, however, told him that wasn't the case. Wade rode with an easy grace, instead of the urgency a crisis would demand.

"Howdy," Grady called out, touching a finger to the brim of his hat.

"Howdy," Wade returned. "Laredo said I'd find you out here. Hope you don't mind that I borrowed one of your geldings."

"I don't have the slightest objection." Wade was a fine rider; if he hadn't become a preacher, Grady figured he would've made one hell of a rancher.

"Have you got a few minutes?" Wade asked.

"Sure."

Wade regarded him seriously. "What I wanted to discuss is private. I'd prefer that it stayed between you and me."

Grady nodded. "If that's the way you want it, then that's how it'll be."

"I appreciate it." Wade met his eyes. "This is difficult to talk about," he began. "I never asked Caroline about the father of her child."

Grady felt his anger rising. "For all intents and purposes, I'm Maggie's father. That's all anyone needs to know."

"I realize that, Grady, and I certainly don't mean to imply anything by asking—but she has a birth father."

"Yes," Grady admitted reluctantly. He couldn't love his six-year-old daughter any more than he already did.

He remembered his initial shock when he'd learned his no-good brother, Richard, was her biological father—when he'd learned that Maggie was the result of a liaison Richard had apparently forgotten. But none of that mattered. Maggie truly was the child of Grady's heart.

There was a time when she wouldn't even look at him, preferring to hide her face in her mother's skirts. Having little experience with children, he'd been unintentionally gruff and impatient with her. But eventually Maggie had been won over—not without determined effort on his part and not without a crisis first. In retrospect he was pleased that winning Maggie's heart had been so difficult. When they'd finally made their peace, he'd experienced a sense of exhilaration and triumph.

"Why all these questions about Maggie?" Grady asked.

Now it was Wade's turn to grow silent for a long moment. "Did you meet Amy Thornton at the dance Saturday night?"

"Amy Thornton," Grady repeated. He frowned. "Isn't she the gal taking the birthing class with Caroline and me?"

"She's the one," Wade said, nodding.

"Dovie's her partner?"

"Yes."

Grady eyed the reverend. "The pretty little gal."

Wade nodded again.

Grady understood now why Wade had come to him.

"Are you planning to ask her to marry you?" he asked bluntly.

Wade eye's widened at the directness of the question. "I can't answer that…"

"But you're thinking about it?"

"Not yet, but…well maybe," he admitted.

For a man contemplating marriage, Grady noticed that Wade didn't seem too pleased. Time for a man-to-man discussion, as his father used to say. That being the case, they might as well sit down and let the horses rest. He headed Starlight in the direction of the creek.

A silent and obviously troubled Wade followed him over the crest of the hill. Willow trees bordered the slow-moving water, their long supple branches dipping lazily in the cool water. Grady dismounted and led Starlight to the creek's sloping bank. He sat on a large rock and waited until Wade was comfortable before he resumed the conversation. "Okay, let's talk this out," he suggested.

"The thing is," Wade said, "I don't *know* anything about Amy."

"Do you love her?" It was a bold question, but Grady couldn't see skirting around the subject when that was all that truly mattered.

Wade's head came up. "I think so… Yes." He closed his eyes. "I don't know why I do or how it happened. A week ago I was doing everything I could, short of leaping off a bridge, to get out of taking her to the dance."

Grady laughed. "I seem to recall Caroline mentioning a certain reluctance on your part."

"You mean Amy knew?"

"I think she might have."

Wade groaned aloud.

"What caused this sudden change of heart?"

The question went unanswered for a moment. "I'd tell

you straight if I could. When I went to pick her up for the dance, I felt as if…as if someone had stuck me with a cattle prod. I'd noticed her before, plenty, but I don't know… I was afraid, I guess. Afraid of exactly what's happening now. She's beautiful, but I don't want you to think that's the only reason I'm attracted to her.''

''Well, it doesn't hurt any.''

''True, but it's much more than that,'' Wade said. He reached for a long blade of grass and peeled off a strip. ''I've only kissed her once, and as far as kisses go, it was pretty chaste.''

''But you enjoyed it.''

Wade's tight face broke into a grin. ''I damn near blew a fuse.''

Grady laughed, remembering the first time he'd kissed Caroline. It had left him reeling for days. All he could think about was kissing her again. Judging by the desperation and yearning on his face, Wade was obviously experiencing the same reaction.

''Then Monday night at Nell's wedding…''

''Yes?'' Grady prodded the minister.

''I…I had the strongest sense—'' he glanced at Grady, then quickly averted his gaze ''—that Amy and I were meant to be together.'' He paled slightly. ''I barely know her and I know almost nothing about her past.''

''You mean, who's the father of her baby and why isn't she with him?'' Grady believed in plain speaking.

Wade shrugged, and again he hesitated. ''It's just that…''

''Just what?''

Wade tossed the blade of grass aside and then, as if he needed something to do with his hands, removed his hat and held it by the brim, slowly rotating it. ''I'm worried,'' he admitted.

"Falling in love isn't always easy," Grady said, feeling adequately knowledgeable on the subject. "Especially when there's a child involved. That complicates things. But you have to be willing to love the kid as if she's your own—or he, of course. And you have to trust the woman you love...." His own romance with Caroline had gone through its share of difficulties. In truth, he'd been a stubborn fool, and it'd probably help Wade if he shared that, but Grady preferred to let Wade think him wise and perceptive.

"There's a lot of unknowns with Amy."

That would worry Grady, too. It'd been different with Caroline. Grady had known her almost all his life, not that he'd paid her any heed until recent years, when she'd become friends with Savannah.

"You might just ask her," Grady said. "I find the direct approach less confusing and troublesome myself."

"I could do that," Wade agreed, but he didn't sound confident about it.

"You don't want to ask her a lot of questions," Grady said.

"I'd rather she volunteered the information."

Grady didn't blame him for that. They sat there a good ten minutes without either one of them speaking. Grady was a patient man; he didn't mind waiting.

But when Wade continued to brood in silence, Grady finally asked, "What can I do to help you?"

Wade seemed to slowly shake himself free of his thoughts. "I guess I want you to tell me I'm not acting like a fool," he said in a low voice. "And that there's a chance for me with Amy—and her baby. That I'll say and do the right things."

Grady stood and slapped the minister on the back. "You'll know what's right when the time comes."

Wade exhaled. "I expect I will. Thanks for the pep talk."

"No problem. Come to me for advice anytime you want. I'm not exactly an expert on romance, but I'm willing to help." He actually felt sorry for the poor guy. He'd known Wade for a long time now and had never seen him looking so confused and unsettled.

Falling in love wasn't all starlit nights and picnics and romantic moments; it was also pain and uncertainty and risk.

Wade had just found that out.

AMY AWOKE BEFORE DAWN on the Fourth of July, excited about spending this day with Wade McMillen.

Admittedly part of her excitement was due to the fact that she'd been invited to join his family's celebration of the holiday. In their brief conversation she'd learned that Wade was the oldest of three. His younger brother and sister were both married and each had two children. His mother apparently doted on her grandchildren.

The thought produced a small stab of pain. Amy's mother had wanted nothing to do with *her* grandchild. With effort Amy pushed away all thoughts of her. Alicia Thornton's life had been ravaged by drugs, alcohol and an endless series of disastrous relationships; she'd never functioned with any adequacy as a parent.

From the time she was able to make sense of her own life, Amy had been determined not to make the same mistakes her mother had. Until recently she'd done a good job, behaving responsibly. Then she'd met Alex.

He was another person she preferred not to think about.

Wanting to contribute something to the festivities, Amy tied an apron around her nightgown. "Okay, Sarah," she said, "we're going to bake Wade an apple pie." Dovie had told her Wade had a sweet tooth and one of his all-time favorites was apple pie. She'd even provided Amy with a recipe from her grandmother's cookbook. A crust made with buttermilk, and a few chopped dates added in with the apples.

Feeling ambitious, Amy baked two pies. One apple and one strawberry-rhubarb. Both turned out beautifully. She left them on the kitchen counter to cool, then showered and dressed for the day.

Her wardrobe was limited, but Savannah had given her a few clothes that fit perfectly. She chose a pair of shorts and a sleeveless top, then glanced at herself in the full-length mirror on the bedroom door.

"Oh, my, Sarah Jane," she whispered when she viewed her reflection. "We look *very* pregnant."

Well, there was no help for that. It wasn't as if she could hide the pregnancy; anyway, Wade was well aware of her condition when he invited her. If he'd had second thoughts, he would have said something before now.

No sooner had she finished curling her hair and applying her makeup than the doorbell chimed.

Wade stood there, looking about as handsome as a man had any right to be. She felt a jolt of pleasure at the sight of him.

"Come on inside," she said, unlatching the screen door. "I'm almost ready."

"I'm a few minutes early."

Amy hadn't noticed. "All I need to do is load up the pies."

"Pies?" He quirked one eyebrow.

"Strawberry-rhubarb and apple."

He groaned. "Apple's my favorite."

"That's what Dovie said."

"Did she also tell you what she discovered with

Frank—that the way to a man's heart is through his stomach?''

Amy unsuccessfully hid a smile. ''She might have mentioned something along those lines.'' She found a cardboard box in which to transport the pies. Wade moved to help her, and before she understood what he was doing, they bumped into each other.

His arm went out to balance her and she froze when his skin touched hers. Slowly she raised her eyes to his. Her breath jammed in her throat at the look of naked longing on his face. And she realized that same longing was reflected on her own.

Without conscious decision—Amy was convinced of that—they reached for each other. Her arms circled his neck and she stood on her toes, offering him her mouth. Wade kissed her with a thoroughness that left her grateful she was supported by his embrace.

''I've been dreaming of kissing you again since last Saturday.''

''I…have, too,'' she whispered. Her eyes were closed. She was afraid to open them, afraid reality would ruin the moment and she couldn't bear that.

''I've thought of nothing but you all week.''

''Oh, Wade, are we crazy? I hardly know you. You hardly know me. And yet…it's as though we're… supposed to be together.''

She felt his chest lift with a sharp intake of breath and instantly regretted having spoken. It was true; she'd thought of him all week. But it'd been more than that. Something had changed the night of Nell and Travis's wedding.

Something had happened. Even though Amy didn't really know the couple, she'd let Dovie persuade her to attend the ceremony. Dovie had explained how Nell and

Travis had met and fallen in love, and she'd mentioned the ghost town. Amy had found their story inspiring and romantic. She had to admit she was intrigued by Bitter End, too. To think the town had been forgotten all those years!

But as she sat in the church, her attention focused on Wade, and she suddenly had the most intense feeling of *connection*. She was going to love Wade McMillen, she knew it, and he was going to love her. She couldn't explain where this certainty had come from, but she'd definitely felt it. And so, she thought at the time, had he.

However, having recently demonstrated her poor judgment when it came to men, Amy wasn't inclined to believe in what had happened. Later she'd managed to convince herself that it had been a form of self-hypnosis. Dr. Jane had said that because of the pregnancy, her emotions might be off-kilter.

That was it, Amy was sure. All these mixed-up feelings had been a fluke. Until now, she'd been able to believe that.

"I'm sorry," she whispered, mortified to the very marrow of her bones. "I didn't mean…"

Wade cradled her face between his hands and gazed into her eyes. "You felt it, too, didn't you?"

She lowered her lashes rather than admit the truth.

He kissed her as though to remove all doubt. This time their kisses were neither patient nor gentle, but fiery. Urgent. She wasn't sure if those kisses were meant to deny what they felt, to prove it false—or the opposite.

The baby stirred and Wade must have felt the movement because he abruptly broke off the kiss. Speechless, they clung to each other.

"We'd better go," he finally said. "We have a long drive ahead of us, and Mom and Dad are waiting."

Amy envied him his fast recovery. By the time the effect of their kisses had worn off, Wade had loaded the pies into his vehicle. Amy grabbed her purse and a sweater and locked the house.

Once they were on the road, Wade turned on the radio and they sang along to a Willie Nelson ballad at the top of their lungs. There was something exhilarating about speeding down the highway on a perfect July morning. Amy felt a delicious sense of anticipation, a quivery excitement.

"Tell me about Bitter End," she said when the song was over.

He seemed surprised that she knew about the abandoned town. "It was settled, oh, about 130 years ago, after the Civil War, by families hoping to make a better life for themselves," he said. "Then…there was some kind of crisis. Nell and Travis found out there'd been an unjust hanging. A preacher's son. Afterward the town was said to be cursed by the preacher, and everyone moved away."

"I'd like to see it."

"I'm sure you will someday."

"It must be an incredible sight," she said, remembering what Dovie had told her, although her friend hadn't actually been to the town herself. Ellie had, but wasn't inclined to speak of it. "Perhaps we could explore it together," Amy suggested.

"Perhaps," he said noncommittally.

"Tell me more about your family," she said next.

"Mom's a housewife-turned-shop-owner," he told her. "After all the years of staying home for us kids, she started her own yarn shop when Janice Marie went away to college. She's always loved to knit, and this seemed a perfect outlet for her creativity. I don't think anyone's more surprised at Mom's success than she is."

''I don't know how to knit.''

''Then my mother would love to teach you—whether you want to learn or not,'' he said with a chuckle. ''Dad's a retired insurance broker, but he's busier now than he ever was working. He volunteers at the grade school tutoring children at risk. Last I heard, he was coaching Little League, too. He told me he simply hasn't got time to work, not when he's having this much fun.''

''It sounds like you have a wonderful family.''

''Just wait until you taste the barbecue. That's Dad's real speciality. He won't let anyone near the grill, not even my mother. He takes real pride in his slow-grilled ribs.'' Wade went on to describe the apron and hat his father would be wearing. A complete wardrobe reserved for the Fourth of July.

Amy's laugh was carefree. ''Now what about your sister?''

''She's mean and ugly.''

''Wade!''

''Well, she was when she was twelve and if she's changed I haven't noticed.''

Amy didn't believe him for a minute.

''I can't understand what prompted André to marry Janice Marie.''

''It might've had something to do with love.''

Wade snickered. ''It might, but I doubt it. Janice Marie bakes the world's best applesauce cake, and André has a weakness for it.''

Amy rolled her eyes.

''Hey, he confessed it to me himself.''

''What about your brother?''

''Larry? He's spoiled rotten. Both him and Janice. I'm the only one who turned out decent.''

''Yeah, right.'' She grinned. ''I can't wait to ask your

mother the *real* story. You know, I'm so looking forward to meeting them.'' She paused. ''What did they say when you told them you were bringing me?'' She leaned back, patting her rounded stomach.

''They don't know you're coming.''

Amy's amusement died. ''What do you mean, they don't know I'm coming?''

Wade didn't appear to notice how upset she was.

''I didn't tell them. Hey, it's no big deal.''

''Yes, it is,'' she said, her panic rising. ''Take me back to Promise,'' she demanded. ''I can't—I *won't* meet your family. Not like this. Not without them knowing…''

Chapter Six

Wade pulled over to the side of the road. Amy looked as if she was about to burst into tears. And he had no idea what he'd done wrong.

"Amy?"

She was breathing hard and tears welled in her eyes. She opened the car door and leaped out.

"What is it?" He followed her, not sure what to do.

"You didn't even tell your parents you'd invited me to the family get-together?"

He gave her a puzzled look. "We often invite impromptu guests. Mom prepares enough food to feed a small army You're welcome with or without my parents' knowledge."

"Then they don't know I'm pregnant, either." She folded her arms and glared at the sky. "That was a stupid question, seeing they don't even know I exist!"

"My parents aren't going to judge you," Wade promised. "They'll be thrilled I'm bringing you."

She didn't seem convinced.

"All right, all right," he said. "If it's that important, then I'll use my car phone and we'll call them from here."

He watched her shoulders rise and then fall with a deep

troubled sigh. "Are you going to tell them I'm almost seven months pregnant, too?"

"Ah…" He hesitated, not sure how to answer. If he admitted he was, Amy might find fault with him for warning his parents. If he reassured her he wasn't going to say a word, she might accuse him of setting them up for a shock. Either way, he feared he'd end up with just enough rope to hang himself. "What would *you* like me to say?" he asked.

"Tell them," she said, then chewed on her lower lip.

"Okay." He sat back in the car and reached for the phone.

He'd punched out four numbers when she cried out, stopping him. "No, don't!"

Wade replaced the receiver. "Maybe we'd better go over exactly what you do want me to say. Rehearse it in advance."

Amy climbed back into the Blazer and sat there, arms crossed. After a long tense moment she glanced at him. "Do you have any suggestions?"

"I could tell them we met in church."

"Well…" Her beautiful eyes smiled once again. "Isn't that a bit deceptive?"

Wade grinned. "It's the truth—sort of."

The amusement fled from her face. "Oh, Wade, I don't know what we should do."

"Couldn't we simply enjoy the afternoon?" That seemed the obvious solution to him.

"But I'll be self-conscious the entire time."

"Because you're pregnant?"

Amy covered her cheeks with both hands. "I can only imagine what your family will think of me."

"What makes you assume they're going to think anything?"

"Because people do. It's only natural."

"Then they'll think I'm the luckiest man alive to have convinced such a beautiful woman to share the Fourth of July with me." His mother and father were kindhearted generous people, but she wouldn't know that until she'd met them. Never in all his life had he seen either of his parents intentionally shun or hurt anyone. They just weren't like that. He wanted to tell Amy, but feared she wouldn't believe him.

"They'll think I'm one of your charity cases," she muttered.

Wade didn't mean to laugh, but the idea was so ludicrous, he couldn't help it.

"I'm glad you find this funny," she said. "Unfortunately, I don't."

His laughter died, and Wade turned to grasp her by the shoulders. "Oh, Amy, you're about as far from being a charity case as it's possible to get."

She blinked. "How do you mean?"

"Every time I look at you, I have to remind myself that I'm a pastor."

She frowned, and he released her.

"Don't you know?" he asked. "Every time I'm with you, I end up fighting with myself because I want…" He dared not finish the sentence, afraid he'd reveal the depth of his feelings. "Every time I'm with you I want to kiss you again," he said, his voice dropping to a whisper.

"Oh, Wade, how can you find me attractive with my stomach like this and…and my feet swollen?"

He smiled, wondering if she honestly didn't know. She was beautiful, so damned beautiful—inside and out. "I've never been more attracted to a woman than I am to you right this minute," he confessed. Gently he brushed the hair from her cheek.

Not to kiss her then would have been a travesty. Before he could question the wisdom of it, he leaned across the seat and pulled her forward for a slow deep kiss. Amy sighed, and her arms went around his neck and she melted against him. Kissing Amy was pure emotion, pure sensation…pure ecstasy. Because he was a minister, he sometimes forgot he was a man, with a man's needs and desires. That was the real reason Dovie had wanted him to start seeing Amy. He understood that now, although he hadn't appreciated her interference at the time. At the moment, however, he didn't need any reminders of his humanness. None whatsoever.

They kissed again and again, until he felt his control slipping. "Amy…" he groaned, needing to break this off while some shred of sanity remained. Already his thinking had become clouded by desire. He pulled away and cleared his throat. "I'm taking you to meet my parents," he said.

Amy didn't argue and Wade was grateful. He started the engine, and after glancing in the rearview mirror, edged the Blazer back onto the highway. "You don't have anything to worry about," he assured her, reaching for her hand. "Mom and Dad are going to love you."

Amy said nothing, but gave him a worried look.

"All I ask…" He hesitated.

"Yes?" she prompted.

"Just remember this is my mother. She's proud of me…"

"Then she won't appreciate someone like me messing up your life. That's what you're trying to tell me, isn't it?"

The pain in her voice hurt him. "No, I was about to ask you not to listen to her tales of how well I took to potty training. That kind of thing."

Obviously relieved, Amy laughed. "She wouldn't say anything like that, would she?"

"I'm afraid so."

The tension eased from her face, and the beginnings of a smile took over.

"Mom dragged out my baby book the last time I brought a woman home for her and Dad to meet. You can't imagine how embarrassing it is to have a woman I'm dating examine naked baby pictures of me."

Amy cast him a skeptical glance. "You do this often, do you? Bring women home for your family to meet?" Her eyes held a teasing glint.

He'd walked into that one with his eyes open. "Well...not exactly."

"When was the last time?"

This was a test of Wade's memory. "It must be four or five years ago."

She raised her eyebrows as though she wasn't sure she should believe him.

"It's true," he insisted. "You can ask Mom yourself if you like." He wanted to let her know how special she was to him.

After almost three hours' driving, they reached Wade's hometown just outside Houston, a small community not unlike Promise.

The second Wade pulled into the driveway, the screen door opened and both his parents came out. His nieces and nephews, whom he loved beyond measure, followed right on their heels.

Wade squeezed Amy's hand. "You're going to be great. You don't have a thing to worry about."

Her smile was brave as Wade helped her out of the car. His parents hugged him briefly, then stepped back and waited for an introduction. Wade scooped up his two nieces and hugged them both, then gave his attention to the two boys.

"Mom, Dad, this is Amy Thornton," he said, his hand on her shoulder. "Amy, my parents, Charles and Karen McMillen."

Both his parents smiled and at precisely the same moment, as though rehearsed in advance, they lowered their eyes to Amy's stomach.

"That's either Sarah or Joseph," Wade continued.

"Good classic names," his mother said, recovering first.

Maybe he should've given them some warning, after all.

"Amy, this is Peter, Paul, Margaret and Mary," Karen McMillen said, gathering her grandchildren around her. "Welcome to our home."

Amy's hands trembled with nerves, Wade saw, but she smiled politely and extended her hand.

"We don't stand much on ceremony here," his mother said. Putting an arm around Amy's waist, she led her toward the house. "Come on inside and I'll introduce you to the rest of the family. Janice and her husband and Larry and his wife are already here."

Wade couldn't remember a time he'd loved or appreciated his mother more. As soon as his mother and Amy were out of earshot, his father cornered him.

"She's pregnant."

Wade grinned. "So I noticed."

"Does someone intend to make an honest woman of her?" his father asked.

Wade's gaze followed Amy and he experienced a rush of emotion. "She's already honest—but I think I'm going to love her and her child."

His father nodded his head vigorously. "Good answer, son. No need to say more."

AMY HAD NEVER KNOWN a family like this, so close and fun-loving, generous and expressive. Because she was new here and still self-conscious, she felt most comfortable observing their interactions from a distance. Everyone treated her in a warm, genuinely friendly way. The kids were full of questions about her and Wade. She answered the ones she could and referred the ones she couldn't to him. Amy immediately liked his brother and sister, especially Janice, who was quick to point out that her name wasn't Janice Marie but Janice Lynn. Apparently only Wade called her Janice Marie. As a six-year-old allowed to help choose a name for his baby sister, he'd been adamant that his parents use Marie. Lynn, he'd insisted, sounded too much like a last name. Wade's younger brother didn't look at all like Wade. He was shorter and heavier set, while Wade was tall and lean. Larry was an insurance broker like his dad had been, and Janice ran a graphic-design business from her home.

More than once Amy found herself drawn into the family's activity, not because anyone tried to persuade her but because of the sheer fun they were having. Karen's grandchildren couldn't wait for dark before lighting their fireworks, so she gave them each a sparkler. Mary, who was just five, was terrified of the sparks and the sputtering, but refused to allow her brother and cousins to know it. She held her arm out as far as possible and squeezed her eyes shut as if she expected the sparkler to explode any second.

Midafternoon Charles McMillen donned his apron and chef's hat and began his stint at the barbecue. He was definitely in charge and very serious about it, too. But he allowed Amy to assist him with basting the ribs and the chicken. She had a wonderful time as they exchanged outrageous jokes and silly remarks. To have had a father like this...

Once dinner was ready, it lasted a full hour. Wade hadn't been exaggerating when he claimed his mother prepared enough food to feed an army; they needed two picnic tables to hold it all.

What amazed Amy most was the laughter and the noise. She didn't know families had this much fun together. The kids raced around the backyard, chasing each other, and if not each other, then butterflies. Games followed, croquet and a hotly contested game of basketball between Wade, his brother and brother-in-law.

"They used to play as boys," Janice said, sitting next to Amy. "Mom used to have to drag them off the court when it was time for supper."

Late in the afternoon Wade and Larry set up a badminton net and insisted everyone had to participate. Amy wasn't sure she'd be an asset, but Wade convinced her to join in.

"But I'm not any good at this." It was too humiliating to confess she'd never played.

"It's easy," he insisted. "Besides, I'll cover for you." He winked as he said it, as though he could actually manage to be in two places at once.

"All right, but don't be mad if I lose the game for us."

"Not to worry, I won't let that happen."

"What line of bull is my brother feeding you?" Janice shouted from the other side of the net.

"My advice is not to listen to him," Wade's brother declared.

Once the game started, Amy was delighted by how much fun it was. They played a sort of free-for-all style, with the children running furiously after each serve, shouting and laughing. The birdie apparently had a mind of its own and flew in every which direction except the one intended. It wasn't long before everyone dissolved into giggles.

At one point the birdie came right toward Amy. Every time it was anywhere close to her, Wade stepped forward and returned it with surprising ease.

Not this time.

"Get it, Amy," he shouted from behind her.

"Me? You want me to get it?" Even as she spoke, she raised her racket. Her shoe must have slid in a damp spot on the grass because her foot went out from under her and she dropped to her knees. Nevertheless, she returned the birdie, but in her enthusiasm lost her balance and fell forward, landing on her chin. The shock was softened by the soft ground, but it jarred her for a moment.

"Amy!" Wade was at her side in an instant. "Are you all right?" He dropped his racket on the grass and helped her sit up.

Amy was shocked to see the fear and concern in his eyes. "I'm fine...really. There's nothing wrong."

"What about your chin? The baby?"

"Everything's fine, Wade." Using his shoulder for leverage, she got back to her feet and reached for her racket.

"I think we should call it quits," Wade said.

His words were followed by a loud chorus of objecting voices, Amy's included.

"We're not going to quit," she insisted. "Not when we're down by two measly points."

"Yeah," ten-year-old Peter said. "I'm not a quitter."

"Me, either," Paul added.

"We're actually ahead?" Larry asked as if this was news to him. "Maybe it isn't such a bad time to quit, after all."

Janice and Larry's wife started swatting him with their

badminton rackets, but it was all in fun. The game ended in a tie a few minutes later, and they all stopped when Karen called them back to the table for dessert.

"Who brought the apple pie?" Larry asked.　Everyone turned to look at Amy in response to Larry's question. She wasn't sure what to say or do.

"It's the best apple pie I've ever tasted," he said, saluting her with his fork. "The crust is fabulous."

"You're eating my pie!" Wade accused him. "Amy baked that for me."

"You aren't going to eat a whole pie," his brother said confidently.

"Who says?"

"Boys, boys," their mother chided.

"I'll bake another," Amy offered.

That seemed to appease Wade. "All right," he said, and sat back down.

"For Larry," Amy added, and the entire family burst out laughing.

All too soon the day was over. Because of the long drive back to Promise, Wade and Amy left before the big fireworks display.

Amy hugged both of Wade's parents on her way out the door. Neither one had asked her embarrassing questions. Instead, they'd opened their home and their hearts to her without making judgments, with acceptance and love.

"Well?" Wade asked, once they were on the road.

She knew what he was asking. "Your family's…wonderful." No single word adequately described the experience of being with such warm gracious people.

"I told you so, didn't I?"

Amy rested her head against the back of the seat. "You're one of those, are you? An I-told-you-so guy."

"Hey, when a man's right, he's right and he deserves

to make sure everyone knows it.'' He growled a he-man sound that made Amy laugh. She felt content and utterly relaxed.

An easy silence fell between them.

''I love it when you laugh,'' he said after a few moments.

Amy smiled at his words. There'd been precious little laughter in her life. She wanted to tell him about her childhood, about the things she'd seen, the ugliness she'd experienced. The bare cupboards and drunken men.... But the day was too beautiful to ruin with talk of such memories.

''I like your sister,'' Amy said, instead.

''Janice Marie...''

''She said that isn't her name.''

''Well, that's the name I'd picked out if Mom had a girl. When they decided against it, I was downright insulted. What kind of name is Janice Lynn, anyway?''

''It's lovely,'' she said, thinking how pleased she'd be to have a friend like Janice. ''Your dad's a hoot, too.''

''He takes after me,'' Wade teased.

They chatted for the next hour, laughing frequently. The ride home was punctuated with plenty of washroom breaks—which Amy found she needed these days. They were stopped at a rest area when she first noticed a flash of color in the night sky.

''Look!'' she cried, pointing.

''That's the fireworks from Brewster,'' Wade commented. ''Would you like to watch for a while?''

''Please.''

Wade helped her onto the hood of his Blazer and joined her. Before long the heavens were bright with bursts of color and exploding stars. Amy oohed and aahed at each one. Wade tucked his arm around her shoulders and she leaned against him. They stayed there watching the fireworks until the very end.

It was almost midnight by the time Wade pulled up in front of her house. She struggled to keep her eyes open, yawning as he escorted her to the door.

"That was the most marvelous day of my life," she said. It was the plain and simple truth, although he had no way of knowing that. "Oh, Wade I'm so glad you insisted I meet your family. They're wonderful."

"Hey, what about me?"

"You're not so bad yourself."

Moonlight dimly lit the small porch, and when Wade smiled down on her she realized how much she wanted him to kiss her. How much she needed his touch. It would be the perfect ending to a perfect day.

It seemed he was thinking the same thing, because he reached for her. Amy closed her eyes and sighed. His kisses were slow and leisurely, expressions of comfort and contentment rather than passion. When it was time for her to go inside, Wade unlocked the door and handed her back the key. Then he smiled at her in the moonlight.

"Thank you, Amy, for spending the day with me."

"No, thank *you*," she said. He'd given her so much.

DOVIE LOVED attending the birthing classes with Amy. She'd learned to breathe right along with her younger friend, and they occasionally practiced together in the evenings or on a slow Sunday afternoon.

"You're getting mighty close to Amy and her baby, aren't you?" Frank said one night after dinner. He carried the dirty dishes to the kitchen counter, then poured them each a cup of freshly brewed coffee.

"Does that worry you?" Dovie asked, joining him at the table. She doubted she could hide the truth from her husband. He knew her far too well. Besides, he was right. If she'd had a child of her own, she would have wanted a daughter like Amy. As the weeks went on Amy had come to trust Dovie more and more. Slowly she'd revealed bits and pieces of her past life; this trust had been extended to others, as well. Wade McMillen had a lot to do with the transformation in the young woman, Dovie felt. They were falling in love and it was wonderful to behold.

Poor Wade, Dovie mused. She almost felt sorry for him. He was so enthralled with Amy he could barely think straight. Amy was no different.

"How many classes do you have left?" Frank asked.

"Just a couple more." Dovie knew he found it difficult that she was away every Monday night, but he'd been a good sport about it. She put dinner in the oven and he ate alone, but when she returned from class, she was eager to share her experiences. He listened patiently while she chatted on and on about what she'd learned.

"When's the baby due?"

"Middle of October," Dovie told him. "And you know that as well as I do."

"Everything's fine with the pregnancy, isn't it?"

"According to Jane, everything appears to be normal. Fortunately Amy's young and healthy."

"Good."

Dovie grinned. Frank had taken a liking to Amy, too, although he wasn't as prone to discuss his feelings as she was.

"It seems to me that Amy should start thinking about getting the nursery ready."

"She's doing the best she can," Dovie said, quick to come to her friend's defense. "Denise Parsons is lending her a bassinet."

"What about a crib?"

"Wade's got that covered."

"Wade's buying her a crib?" Frank sounded shocked.

"Not exactly. He found a used one at a garage sale a couple of weeks ago and he's refinishing it."

"Our pastor?"

Dovie couldn't have disguised her delight to save her soul. "Although when it comes to Amy, I sincerely doubt Wade is thinking of her in terms of being her pastor." Dovie finished her coffee. "And I, for one, am thrilled."

"Uh, Dovie, not everyone appreciates Amy the way you and I do," Frank said, not looking directly at her.

"You mean there's been talk about Amy and Wade?"

Frank gave a noncommittal shrug. "Some."

Dovie was furious. "I can't just imagine who's responsible for *that*," she muttered. No one got her dander up faster than Louise Powell. Try as she might to maintain a Christian attitude toward the other woman, Dovie was confronted again and again by her vicious tongue. "What's Louise saying?"

"Well, according to her, there are plenty of women without a questionable past. Wade could be dating them."

Dovie rolled her eyes rather than dignify such a statement with a response.

Frank grinned. "What's fun is watching Louise try to turn folks against Amy. People refuse to listen. They change the subject or make comments like how nice it is to see Wade so happy."

Dovie was proud of their townsfolk, too. "I'm having a baby shower for Amy next week." Everyone she'd called had been eager to participate. "It's a surprise, Frank Hennessey, so don't you let the cat out of the bag, understand?"

"My lips are sealed."

Dovie stood, and her husband grabbed her around the waist and pulled her into his lap.

Dovie put up a token protest, which he ignored.

"Is Amy going to ask us to be the baby's godparents, Dovie?"

"That's up to her." But Dovie strongly suspected she would. Twice now Amy had asked Dovie about the responsibilities entailed and hinted that Dovie and Frank would make wonderful godparents.

Dovie loved Amy's unborn baby as if Sarah or Joseph were her own grandchild. The closer Amy's due date drew, the more excited Dovie became. Already she'd knitted two blankets and one cap-and-bootie set. Her fingers weren't as nimble as they'd once been, but that didn't stop her.

"Sometimes I think…" Dovie paused.

"What?"

She wasn't sure she should say it aloud, but she'd ventured this far. "Sometimes it feels as if Amy is *our* child. She needs a family, and we have all this love to share."

Frank's arms tightened around her waist. "I'm beginning to believe the same thing."

WADE HAD NEVER BEEN good at carpentry. He still recalled his school shop project—a birdhouse. It had been a disaster. Give him a textbook and a room full of students any day of the week. He could teach them the principles of architecture, but he couldn't tell a screwdriver from a wrench.

He didn't know what had made him think he could refinish a crib, but he'd taken on the task with enthusiasm. Amy only worked part-time at the feed store, so once she'd paid her utility bills and bought groceries, she didn't have a lot of money left. The crib was his contribution. His own personal "welcome to the world" gift.

While the refinishing job might not win any awards for skill, he figured he should get an *A* for effort. He'd originally intended to give the crib to Amy at the surprise baby shower Dovie was throwing that afternoon. But it didn't make sense to haul the crib over to Dovie's and then back to Amy's place.

So he did the logical thing. He pretended to know nothing about the shower and dropped it off at her house directly.

Fortunately the contraption folded and fit in the back of his Blazer. Amy was busy washing dishes when he arrived. She wore the same shorts outfit she'd worn the Fourth of July, which produced a rush of warm memories.

"Hi." He kissed her lightly, then followed her inside. "I've got something for you."

"You do?" She smiled with anticipation.

"Sit down and close your eyes." He nudged her into a living-room chair.

Amy sat there quietly, eyes closed as he requested, and while she waited, he returned to the Blazer and carried the crib into the house.

"Okay, you can look now," he said, standing proudly by his work.

Amy stared up at him and then at the crib. Her eyes grew huge. "Oh, Wade." Her hands flew to her mouth.

"I refinished it myself." He realized he sounded like a Cub Scout boasting about his latest achievement badge, but he couldn't help it.

"Now all I need is a screwdriver to, uh, finish tightening the rails." Did that make any sense? He wasn't sure.

"I...don't know if I have one," she said.

Wade let her go through the motions of searching. He'd made darn sure she *didn't* have one before he'd brought the crib over. It was all part of the elaborate plan to get Amy to Dovie's place for the shower.

"Frank must have a screwdriver," he said, reaching for the phone. He went through a little performance at his end—quite convincing if he did say so himself—then hung up. "He wants us to come over."

"When?" Amy asked.

"Now."

She sighed, and he was afraid she might decline with some excuse. "Come on," he urged. "It'll do you good to get out of the house."

She didn't seem to believe him, but finally she nodded and got her purse from the bedroom. At almost eight months pregnant, Amy didn't move around as quickly or comfortably these days.

He helped her into the Blazer and closed the passenger door. He wanted to suggest that she run a comb through her hair or add a touch of lipstick, but didn't dare for fear she'd guess something was up.

"What are all the cars doing at Dovie's house?" she asked.

"I think one of her neighbors is having a Tupperware party," Wade said. Okay, so he was known to stretch the truth now and then. Hey, he wasn't perfect.

He rang the doorbell and stepped aside so Amy would enter the house first.

The instant she did, a loud chorus of "SURPRISE!" greeted her.

She gasped and stumbled back, crashing into him. "You knew?" she asked, twisting around to look at him. Shock and delight flashed from her eyes.

She shook her head. "No one's ever done anything like this for me before," she said, and burst into tears.

Chapter Seven

Four weeks. One month. And then, this tiny being in Amy's womb would be in her arms. It didn't seem possible.

Dressing for her appointment with Dr. Jane, Amy rubbed body lotion over her extended belly. It seemed to stretch halfway across the room. Studying her reflection in the mirror, Amy felt grotesque and misshapen, barely able to believe that this would soon be over. That soon, she'd be holding her baby.

She'd just finished pulling on a dress and slipping into her shoes—she'd long since lost sight of her feet—when the doorbell rang. Wade had wanted to take her to the doctor's appointment. He was even more attentive now, more solicitous. Increasingly Amy had come to rely on him. He was so gentle with her. Lately when they kissed, he restrained himself with two or three chaste kisses. If it wasn't for the yearning she read in his eyes, she might have assumed he no longer found her attractive. His gaze told her otherwise.

"You ready?" he asked, and walked into the living room.

"I'll only be a moment," she promised. "I want to put on some lipstick."

"You're perfect just the way you are."

Amy found his words touching. "You must be at the age where you need glasses, Wade McMillen."

"My eyesight is twenty-twenty," he countered. "I happen to recognize a beautiful woman when I see one."

Amy didn't know what she'd done to deserve someone like Wade in her life. She knew she'd fallen deeply in love with him, and it had become more and more difficult to hide the depth of her feelings. They hadn't spoken of love. Not once. And seeing that she was about to give birth to another man's child, Amy didn't feel she was in any position to discuss her feelings.

"Mom phoned last night," Wade told her. "She wanted to see how you're feeling. She asked me to give you her love."

"I hope you gave her mine," she said on her way into the bathroom.

"I did," Wade called after her.

Amy stood in the front of the mirror and applied a pale rose shade of lipstick. It never ceased to amaze her that a woman who was little more than a stranger would send her love, while her own mother had abandoned her. At no time in the past three months had Alicia Thornton made any attempt to contact Amy. Her mail continued to be forwarded and other than a couple of cards from people at her old job, there'd been nothing. No one had tried to reach her. Not her mother. Not Alex.

Which was just as well. She'd left Dallas wanting to escape their influence and make a new life for herself and her child. She liked the people of Promise and they had welcomed her with kindness and generosity. In only a few months Promise felt more like home than any place she'd ever lived.

DR. JANE PATTERSON'S office had grown steadily busier over the past two months; today the reception room was almost full. Jenny asked Amy to have a seat and Wade sat with her, holding her hand. Her free hand rested on her stomach.

"Would you like to go for lunch later?" he asked.

As often as they saw each other, they rarely went out on what would be considered a date. "I'd like that," Amy said.

"Any cravings?" he murmured. "Pickles? Ice cream?"

"Cheese enchiladas."

"Done. The Mexican Lindo has some of the best."

Amy didn't realize how hungry she was until he'd mentioned food, and then it was all she could think about.

Jenny appeared a minute later. "Amy, Dr. Jane will see you now."

Amy stood. "I'm sure this won't take long," she told Wade.

Jenny took her blood pressure and pulse and entered the numbers on her chart. Amy sat on the end of the examination table and waited.

Dr. Jane came into the cubicle and read the chart. "How are you feeling?" she asked.

"Ambitious," Amy said. She'd gotten the bedroom ready for the baby in the week since her last visit. The gifts from the baby shower had spurred her into activity. Everyone had been so generous.

"Ambitious," Jane repeated. "That's a promising sign. Are you experiencing any problems?"

"You mean other than rolling over in the middle of the night? I feel like a turtle who's been flipped onto its back and can't get up."

Jane grinned. "Other pregnant women have told me the same thing." She checked the swelling in Amy's ankles and after a brief physical exam asked her to make an appointment for the following week.

"Everything okay?" Wade asked Amy once they were outside.

"Perfect," she assured him. Other than feeling ungainly, she'd rarely been in better shape. This could be attributed to the care she'd taken with diet and the number of hours of sleep she seemed to require every night. In addition, Wade and Dovie had pampered her at every turn. Their emotional support and friendship had made a world of difference to Amy, and to the pregnancy.

"You've got my mouth watering for Mexican food," he said, holding her hand firmly in his.

"Mine, too."

They entered the restaurant in a festive mood, and the proprietor himself escorted them to a table. Amy barely had time to open her menu when the waiter appeared with chips, salsa and glasses of water.

"I don't know why I'm bothering to read this," she said. "I already know what I want."

For a moment Amy didn't think Wade had heard her. His attention was focused on the booth directly across from them. Amy's gaze followed his to two middle-aged women, both of whom were more than a little overdressed for the restaurant. One wore a shiny silver running outfit with high heels and star-shaped sunglasses. The other seemed decked out for the beach, in a halter top, panama hat and short shorts. She recognized the woman in silver by sight. Louise Somebody. Dovie had pointed her out; she'd said little, but Amy could tell from her tight-lipped expression that this Louise was not a person she liked or respected.

The waiter returned, ready to take their order and it seemed no time at all before he was back with their meals.

Amy forked up a mouthful, for her first taste. The enchilada was full of spicy refried beans and melted cheese. Mmm. She took a bite, expecting to be transported to culinary heaven. But as soon as her mouth closed around the fork, those expectations were shattered by the conversation at the booth across the aisle.

"It doesn't seem fitting, does it, Tammy Lee, to have our pastor—a man who's supposed to be above reproach—dating an unwed mother."

"Yes, I would've thought Reverend McMillen would show a bit more discretion," the other woman said.

Amy saw Wade stiffen.

"This food is wonderful," Amy said, hoping to distract him and at the same time hide how much those cruel words hurt.

Wade's attention returned to her. "Ignore those two."

"I will if you will," she whispered back.

He nodded.

"She looks like she's about to pop any minute," the one in the beachwear said, just loudly enough to be heard.

"Personally I think Wade's involvement reflects poorly on the entire church." The woman in the running suit didn't bother to hide the fact that she was staring in their direction.

"I'm sure more than one person has questioned his priorities lately."

"Just who is she, anyway?"

Amy set her fork aside, certain she wouldn't be able to swallow another bite. The food that had been so appealing had little flavor now. What the woman said was true—and something Amy had chosen to overlook all these many weeks. Wade was a minister, a man of God; he had a reputation to consider, and his affiliation with her was hurting him in the eyes of his community.

"It's just not what you'd expect from a pastor."

"It makes you wonder…"

Wade slammed his fork down on the table. "I've had enough," he told Amy.

"No, please!" She was embarrassed enough. Anything he said or did would only add to her humiliation. And his own.

Amy had never seen him angry, not like this. His face was white, his fists clenched, as he got out of the booth and approached the two women.

"Good afternoon, Louise. Tammy Lee."

Both women nodded coolly.

"I couldn't help overhearing you just now."

"You heard?" Louise murmured as though she felt shocked by that—although she'd obviously intended it all along. But why? Amy wondered. Why would she purposely set out to embarrass Wade?

"You were talking about Amy Thornton and me. Have either of you met Amy?"

Amy felt their eyes shift to her. She smiled weakly and nodded in their direction.

"No…" one of them said.

"I can't say I've had the…pleasure," the other said.

"I already knew the answer before I asked," Wade confessed wryly, "because if either one of you had made the effort to know Amy, you'd realize something very important."

Both women stared at him.

"Amy is one of the kindest women I've ever known. She'd never go out of her way to embarrass someone—unlike certain others I could mention."

Louise pursed her lips at this.

"Furthermore," Wade continued, "I happen to be very much in love with Amy Thornton."

The shocked gasp, Amy realized, came from her.

"It hurts me that two women who are part of my church family would be this thoughtless, this judgmental. I hope that, in time, you'll both come to know and care about Amy, too."

Amy didn't hear the rest of the conversation. Her thoughts whirled around in her head. *Wade loved her.* He'd admitted it to those two women. But it troubled her that his love for her was damaging his reputation.

She folded her arms beneath her breasts, cradling her child, protecting him or her from the harsh judgments of the world. This matter of seeing Wade socially had worried her before, but they'd never discussed it. She'd been afraid to confront the issue, afraid that once she did, everything would change. Now she saw that her selfishness had hurt him. These women, gossipmongers or not, were members of his church, and it wouldn't be long before word spread throughout the congregation, possibly the entire town.

Reverend Wade McMillen was in love with an unwed mother.

Her thoughts distracted her, and she didn't even notice that Wade had returned to the booth.

"I apologize, Amy," he murmured. "I wish I could have spared you that."

She tried to reassure him with a smile, but was unable to muster even a token effort.

"I'm the one who should apologize."

"Nonsense."

She couldn't stop looking at him, couldn't stop hearing his words. "You love me?" she asked, her voice more breath than sound.

He reached for her hand. "Funny I should admit how I feel about you to someone else first, isn't it?"

"No." Her throat felt thick, clogged with tears, making

it difficult to speak. She lowered her head, trying to clear her thoughts.

"I didn't intend to ask you to marry me like this."

Amy slowly raised her head. "Marry you? But…you don't know anything about me, about my family—about my background."

"I know everything I need to know."

"What about…Sarah? You don't know about her—about the man who fathered her." Amy hadn't mentioned a word about Alex, not to Wade, not to Dovie. Not to anyone. As much as possible, she tried to push every thought of her ex-lover from her mind and heart. One night just recently she'd found herself pretending Wade was Sarah's father, but decided that was a dangerous game.

"I love you, Amy."

"No." She shook her head vigorously. "You don't know what you're saying. You… We've been seeing too much of each other," she said, struggling to hide the panic rising inside her.

"I've never been more certain of anything in my life."

"Oh, Wade." She took her napkin and crumpled it with both hands.

"I want us to get married. Soon, too, so I can be Sarah's daddy."

Amy gave up the effort. She covered her face, reminding herself that her hormones were all askew and not to worry if she was more emotional than usual.

"Is that a yes or a no?" he asked with such gentle concern it made her want to weep.

Fighting for composure, Amy swallowed back tears and inhaled deeply. "I don't know what to say," she managed once her throat muscles had loosened enough for her to speak.

"Say you'll marry me."

"I...need time."

"Darling, I hate to pressure you, but all we've got is a few weeks before we're parents."

She'd love Wade McMillen to her dying day, Amy decided right then and there, for declaring himself Sarah's father.

"I promise to think about it," she told him. For now, that was all she would do. Think. Try to figure out what was best for her and for the baby.

And what was best for Wade.

GRADY, CAL AND GLEN met on the border of Grady's property and the Patterson's ranch, in the same spot they'd often congregated as teenagers. Those days were long behind them now.

"What's this all about?" Cal asked, dismounting as he spoke.

"I assume there's a *reason* you wanted us to meet you here," Glen added, sliding down from his horse, a high-spirited gelding who pranced in place.

While he might sound like he was complaining, Grady could see that his eyes were alight with interest.

Grady grinned at his two best friends. "Actually there *is* an important reason. I want the three of us to return to Bitter End."

"But why? We were there not long ago. Wade was with us, remember? We had a little ceremony, prayed and everything. I'd hoped that was the end of it."

"This is a joke, right?" Glen said irritably.

If Grady hoped to get his friends' attention, he'd achieved his goal.

"No joke," he insisted. "The three of us need to go back."

"I'd like to remind you again that we were just there," Cal muttered.

Grady knew what his friends were thinking, because the same thoughts had been going around in his mind for a number of weeks now.

"Prayer or no prayer, I've seen enough of Bitter End to last me a lifetime," Glen said. "Far as I'm concerned, someone should burn that place to the ground before anyone else gets hurt."

"Then cover it with sulfur," Cal put in.

No one had come away from Bitter End with pleasant memories, not in more than a hundred years. Through research and a good deal of luck, Nell and Travis had uncovered the source of the trouble. Together they'd learned that Bitter End had been cursed by a preacher whose son had been wrongfully hanged. No one had paid much attention to the preacher, but then the town was beset with plagues of the sort brought down on Egypt thousands of years before. The citizens of Bitter End had endured it all—drought and locusts, sickness and hail—until the death of their firstborn children, and then they'd scattered in panic. A number of families from Bitter End had become the founders of Promise.

"Bitter End is a piece of Texas state history," Grady told his friends. "It's a part of who *we* are, as well."

Neither Cal nor Glen was as quick to argue now, and Grady knew it was because they recognized the truth of what he'd said.

"You want us to go back and...and confront the past, don't you?" Cal asked.

"That's my thought," Grady admitted. "I want us to stand in the center of that town and face whatever's there." Grady felt instinctively that this was necessary, although he couldn't really say why.

"We stood there with Wade," Glen pointed out.

"I know...but this is different."

"How?" Cal demanded. Even as he argued, he remounted Thunder, ready to follow through with the idea.

"I want to declare this land free of the curse."

"Like anyone's going to listen to us," Glen said.

"Any*thing,* in this instance," Cal added.

"Whatever." Grady had thought long and hard about this moment. He'd been one of the people who stood with Wade McMillen in the center of Bitter End. One of the men whose roots were buried deep in the history of this forgotten settlement. He wanted whatever was there, the curse, to leave.

They rode in silence, the three of them, like gunfighters heading for a high-noon shoot-out.

The town lay nestled in a small valley below a series of limestone outcroppings. Buildings, both stone and wood, stretched on both sides of the main road. The tallest structure was the church with its burned-out steeple. The wooden two-story hotel, rotting from years of abandonment, leaned precariously to one side, as if the next windstorm would send it toppling. His brother had nearly died in that hotel not many months ago. A sadness came over Grady when he thought of Richard, but he refused to allow his plans to be sidetracked.

By tacit agreement the three men stopped outside the building that had once been the mercantile. The horses shifted restlessly, their acute senses responding to the mysterious atmosphere.

"It's dead here," Glen commented. Nothing grew in town. Bitter End had died all those years ago.

"Do you feel anything?" Cal asked, whispering.

"I'm not sure," Grady said in a normal voice. He refused to give in to whatever was here, refused to bow to his fears.

Glen just looked around, his horse making an abrupt circle as if to check behind himself.

As boys, when they'd first happened upon Bitter End, they'd felt a sense of great sadness, a sense of unease, a tension that manifested itself in the physical. The oppressive silence had frightened them so badly it'd taken them twenty years to venture down these streets again.

The horses seemed incapable of standing still. All three men had trouble restraining them.

"I don't know what I feel," Grady reported. The first time around there'd been no question. The sensation had been overwhelming, unmistakable.

"That feeling of...grief. It's still here," Glen said, glancing over his shoulder. "But not nearly as strong as before."

"I feel it, too." This came from Cal.

"Are you ready to go back now?" Glen's question was directed at Grady.

He nodded, wishing he knew what to do. He'd hoped...hell, he wasn't sure what he'd been hoping for. He supposed he'd wanted to find something different, discover that the town had miraculously changed. That it had—somehow—come back to life.

WADE HAD BEEN looking forward to this for two weeks. Grady and Caroline had invited Amy and him to dinner at the Yellow Rose Ranch. Unfortunately he suspected that if they hadn't already agreed to this, Amy would've found an excuse to decline.

She hadn't been herself since the confrontation with Louise Powell and Tammy Lee Kollenborn in the Mexican Lindo. For the past few days, she'd been quiet and withdrawn, and he knew she was disturbed by what had happened. He didn't blame her.

It didn't help that his marriage proposal had come about the way it had. He'd been trying to work out the best approach all week, but then the incident at the restaurant had forced his hand. It wasn't how he'd wanted to ask her—and he couldn't help feeling some resentment, unchristian though he knew that was, toward those two meddling women.

He glanced at Amy as he drove to the Yellow Rose Ranch. She looked half-asleep, and while he knew she was tired, he also knew she was using her fatigue as an excuse to avoid a certain subject. His proposal. He'd waited a long time to find the woman he wanted to marry, and now he had, he wanted to marry her. The sooner, the better, for the baby's sake, as well as his own.

He wouldn't pressure her into a decision. When she was ready, she'd tell him; until then he'd be patient.

Amy straightened when he turned off the highway and into Grady's long drive. "We're going to have a good time tonight," he promised, leaning over to squeeze her hand.

Amy smiled. "I hope Caroline didn't go to a lot of trouble."

Wade knew Amy's due date was only a week earlier than Caroline's. The two women had become friendly and often met for lunch. He was well aware that Amy admired Caroline and relied on her advice, which Wade saw as a good thing.

Grady stepped onto the porch when Wade steered the Blazer into the yard, and Caroline appeared at her husband's side almost immediately afterward. She hugged Amy, then greeted Wade with real warmth. He gave her the flowers he'd brought in appreciation for the dinner. No wine, not until after the babies were born. He hoped there'd be many more such evenings—some of them at his house. His and Amy's.

It would be just the four of them tonight, since Maggie was spending the night with Savannah.

"Everything's ready," Caroline told them, "so we can eat anytime."

"I'm dying to see your nursery," Amy said.

The two women disappeared, but Wade wasn't fooled. Amy might want to look at the baby's room—he was sure she did—but the real reason she'd gone off with Caroline was to talk to her, perhaps seek out her advice about his marriage proposal.

Wade trusted Caroline to encourage Amy to marry him. If she mentioned what had happened with Louise and Tammy Lee, then Caroline would tell her those two didn't speak for the community. With few exceptions, the entire town had rallied around Amy. Caroline knew that as well as anyone.

In every problem is a gift, his grandfather had told him years ago, and Wade remembered it now. The gift Louise and Tammy Lee had given him was the courage to admit, openly and publicly, that he loved Amy.

Dinner proved to be both relaxing and fun. Caroline was an excellent cook and the prime rib, accompanied by garden fresh broccoli, a green salad and mashed potatoes, was one of the best Wade had tasted. This night out was exactly what he and Amy needed. Conversation was mostly light and entertaining, although they talked about Bitter End and answered Amy's questions. She asked about visiting the town, but both Grady and Wade discouraged that.

While Caroline and Amy cleared the table, Wade and Grady had time to talk privately on the porch.

"Speaking of Bitter End, I was there this week," Grady surprised him by saying.

"What made you go back?" Wade asked, taking a sip of his coffee.

Grady shrugged. "I don't know, but I felt I had to—that there's something unfinished there."

"What?"

"I don't know," Grady said. Then he changed the subject abruptly. "How are things between you and Amy?"

"I love her." Wade had already admitted it once and found it easier the second time.

Grady gave him a slow satisfied smile. "I guessed as much."

"Oh, yeah?"

"'Fraid so, Preacher."

"I've asked her to marry me," Wade confessed.

"Is she going to?"

"I don't know." Wade had promised himself he wouldn't pressure her, but he had a feeling deep in his gut that told him the longer she kept him waiting, the less likely she was to agree. His chest ached at the thought of what his life would be like without her. Every conscious reflection included her. She'd become a big part of his world, of the way he planned his future.

Grady commiserated, but had no advice to offer other than "Don't give up."

At the end of the evening, Amy hugged both Caroline and Grady to thank them for dinner. "I've enjoyed myself so much," she said with such sincerity that no one could doubt her. Least of all Wade.

"Dinner was superb," Wade told Caroline. "Great food, terrific company." Because he was single, he was invited out to dinner quite a bit. No fool he, Wade often accepted. But this evening had shown him what his life would be like if—when—he was married.

Wade waited until they were back on the road before

he broached the subject of marriage. "I wasn't going to say anything," he began, keeping his eyes on the road.

"About what?" Amy asked, then turned to him, eyes filled with alarm. "If you let me sit through the entire evening with a piece of broccoli stuck between my teeth, I swear I'll never forgive you."

Wade chuckled. "It isn't that." His humor quickly faded. "I wanted to ask if you're still thinking about..."

"If I'll marry you," Amy finished for him. "That's what you want to know, isn't it?"

"I love you, Amy. I want to marry you."

She was silent for so long he wondered if he'd blown it entirely. "Say something," he urged, trying not to sound as anxious as he felt.

"His name's Alex Singleton," she said, her voice low. "We met, of all places, in the grocery store."

Wade gripped the steering wheel hard. He wanted to tell her it didn't make a bit of difference who'd fathered her baby. It wasn't a detail he considered necessary. He loved her and he loved her baby. That was the only fact she needed to consider.

It hurt, too, to hear about another man wanting her, making love to her. But he kept his mouth shut, knowing Amy needed to tell him. In some ways this wasn't for him as much as it was for her.

"He asked me out for coffee. I said no, but he was charming and funny and persistent, so I agreed. The store had a deli, and we sat there. We...talked so long that the ice cream in my cart melted." She smiled at the memory. "He was sophisticated and wonderful. I thought I was in love that first day."

Wade found that listening was more difficult by the minute.

"Because he often went away on business, we weren't

able to see each other more than once a week. I...I lived for those weekly dates. Regular as clockwork, he arrived every Wednesday evening and took me out to dinner. We ate at the most wonderful restaurants. Small upscale places.''

''So he had lots of money.''

''Oh, he had more than that, Wade.'' Her voice hardened. ''He also had a wife and two children.''

Chapter Eight

Thursday afternoon, Ellie Patterson left the feed store early. George, her assistant, would close up and Amy would help him. Amy had been taking on more responsibilities of late, and Ellie was grateful. She hadn't been feeling well the past couple of afternoons but suspected she knew why—especially since the home pregnancy test had been positive. Seeing her sister-in-law would confirm what she already knew.

Jenny Bender, Jane's receptionist, was just leaving when Ellie entered the health clinic.

"Jane's in her office," Jenny told her, motioning beyond the reception area.

"Thanks."

Sure enough, Jane sat at her desk making notations on a chart. She glanced up when she heard Ellie come in, and her tired face brightened. "Hi, there."

"Hi." Ellie threw herself into the chair nearest Jane's.

"Long day?" Jane asked sympathetically.

"Exceptionally long."

"You're looking a little peaked."

"I feel a little peaked."

Jane studied her. "Do you think you picked up a bug?"

A slow happy smile came from deep within. "The nine-month variety."

Surprise showed in Jane's face. "You're pregnant?"

Ellie nodded. "The little stick turned blue."

Jane clapped her hands in delight. She closed the chart she'd been working on and relaxed in her chair. "Does Glen know?"

"Not yet." Ellie hadn't meant to keep it a secret from her husband, but she didn't want him to be disappointed if it turned out, for some reason, to be a false alarm. "I thought I'd have you verify my condition first."

They chatted for a few minutes, laughed about the things they always did and made plans to spend a weekend in San Antonio later in the month. They talked with the easy familiarity that had developed between them since they'd married the Patterson brothers. Not until after Jane had examined her did Ellie grow quiet.

Jane didn't press her, but Ellie knew her sister-in-law was waiting for her to speak. "I'm afraid, Jane," she confessed. Her emotions had never been this muddled. Intertwined with the joy were all the fears she'd tried to ignore and couldn't.

"It's normal to be anxious. This is your first child, and your body's experiencing quite a few changes, right now. That can be confusing and stressful. Let's talk about it."

Ellie took a deep breath. "Mostly I'm worried that I'll be like my mother. She didn't have an easy pregnancy with me—that's basically why I'm an only child. And she never seemed to *like* having a kid around." Ellie hadn't been close to her mother, but the bond she'd shared with her father had been strong and special. It was the reason his death the previous year had shaken her so badly.

"You're not your mother," Jane assured her.

Ellie relaxed a little. "In other words, don't borrow trouble?"

"That's a good place to start."

Ellie nodded. "You're right. And I don't think my mother ever wanted a child, whereas I do." She gave Jane a tremulous smile. "Glen and I talked about starting our family soon. That's the reason I went off the pill when I did," she confided, "but we didn't think it'd happen so quickly."

"So you're not sure you're ready for this."

Ellie thought about that for a moment. "No, I'm ready," she said decisively. "I just hadn't expected to be this…fertile."

"I imagine Glen's going to gloat to Cal," Jane said with a manufactured groan.

"Have you and Cal decided when you're going to get pregnant?" Ellie felt it would be nice if their children were close in age. Her own cousins, who'd lived in Brewster, were twins, two years older, and when they were around, it was almost like having brothers. Her mother blamed her tomboy attitudes on Rick and Rob, both of whom had gone on to make the military their career. They'd missed her wedding, but had written to congratulate her and Glen.

"Before Cal and I can think about a family, I need to fulfill my contract here at the clinic," Jane said with a show of regret. "Don't misunderstand me, I love my work. It's just that we're eager to become parents. We're hoping I'll get pregnant about this time next year."

"That'd be wonderful."

"Mary's going to be pleased when she hears your news," Jane said, referring to their mother-in-law.

Glen's parents were looking forward to becoming grandparents, and it went without saying that they'd be ecstatic.

"I want you to start prenatal vitamins right away—"

"Jane, Jane." Ellie held up her hand. "Don't treat me like a patient. I'm your sister-in-law."

Jane laughed. "You're right. Congratulations!" She stood up and hurried over to Ellie to share a heartfelt hug.

FRIDAY MORNING Wade knew he should be working on his sermon, but he couldn't focus his thoughts. Every time he started to write down an idea, all he could think about was Amy. He worried about her, worried that she wasn't eating properly or getting enough rest. He wished she could take a few weeks off before the birth. He wondered what plans she'd made for child care once her maternity leave ended.

Now that her due date was so close, his worrying had become almost obsessive. If she wouldn't marry him, then he hoped she'd at least allow him to be with her when Sarah was born.

When he'd spoken to her on the phone recently, she hadn't sounded particularly interested in his company. But that could be his own doubts talking, because when he showed up at the house yesterday, she'd seemed genuinely pleased to see him.

Wade stared down at his sermon notes and, feeling uninspired, decided to take a break. His first inclination was to head for the feed store, check up on Amy, but he refused to make a pest of himself.

The one person who was sure to understand how he felt was Dovie Hennessey. Dovie was close to Amy, her birthing partner. He had another reason for visiting Dovie's store; he wanted to buy a gift, for Amy, a robe for after the baby was born. Something lovely and feminine.

He walked from the church into town, stopped to chat with the Moorhouse sisters en route. He arrived at Dovie's to find her, as usual, doing a robust business. She acknowl-

edged his presence with a nod and continued to help Betty
Bonney, who was considering an antique bowl and pitcher
for her guest bedroom.

Wade was a patient man. While he was waiting, he wandered around Dovie's store, picturing Amy wearing this
necklace or that scarf, imagining her on the brocade-
upholstered love seat, holding her baby. With him beside
her....

A while later Mrs. Bonney left smiling and Dovie turned
her attention to Wade. "This is a pleasant surprise," she
said. "What can I do for you, Pastor?"

"It's about Amy," he replied, feeling a bit self-
conscious. "I wanted to buy her something to wear after
the baby's born. A robe. Or whatever you think would be
appropriate." Actually this was all mildly embarrassing.
He could just imagine what Louise Powell would say if
she heard about this. If the woman thought it improper for
him to have lunch with Amy, what would she think about
his buying her nightwear? It didn't *matter* what Louise
thought, he chided himself. She was an uncharitable and
narrow-minded woman, and her opinions were of no con-
sequence.

"A robe is an excellent choice." Dovie beamed him an
approving look. "It's both practical and luxurious."

He nodded. "I want it to be special—not the type of
robe she'd wear every day...if you know what I mean."

"I do. In fact, I have something in mind," Dovie said
with a satisfied smile. "I was actually thinking of giving
this to Amy myself." She led him to the far side of her
shop. A selection of old-fashioned wardrobes dominated
one corner. The doors of one wardrobe were open to reveal
a number of party dresses and nightgowns on scented
hangers. She reached inside and pulled out a soft pink satin

robe, its long sleeves and collar edged in lace. It was exactly what he'd hoped for. Simple, elegant, beautiful.

"It's new—not vintage," Dovie explained. "But it's modeled after a 1930s pattern." She watched for his reaction. "What do you think?"

He swallowed hard and nodded. The vision of Amy in that robe did funny things to his insides. "It's perfect."

"I agree," Dovie said. "It's utterly feminine and I know she'd treasure it."

Wade touched the sleeve, intending to look at the price tag, but changed his mind the instant his hand made contact with the rich smooth fabric. His gut clenched. Amy, wearing this. Lying in his bed...

"I'll take it," he said quickly.

"Don't you want to know the price?" Dovie asked.

"Not particularly."

Dovie's grin spread across her face.

Wade took out his wallet as he and Dovie walked toward the cash register. She wrapped the robe in tissue paper and placed it carefully in a gift box, which she tied with a pink ribbon. When she'd finished, she glanced up at him. "Amy told you about Alex, didn't she?" Her gaze held his.

"Yes."

"She only told me this week, you know. She's shared very little about the baby's father."

"It's not important." He wanted Dovie to know he hadn't asked. In fact, he'd almost rather Amy hadn't told him.

"After the birthing class this week, I brought her home for tea. She cried her eyes out."

"Amy was upset?" He wasn't sure what unnerved him more— Amy's being distressed enough to cry or her choosing to weep on Dovie's shoulder and not his.

"Yes. She told me about Alex—and about her relationship with you. She said you'd been wonderful."

That reassured him a little; Amy must still care for him, still trust him. Her story had broken his heart. Yes, she'd been foolish and naive, but she wasn't the first woman who'd learned such lessons the hard way. Not the first woman who'd been lied to by a married man—and fallen in love with him.

"You love her, don't you?" Dovie asked, then laughed at her question. "You must. No man pays $125 for a satin robe otherwise."

Wade gasped in mock outrage. He would gladly have paid twice that.

"Do you want me to keep it here at the store for you until the baby's born?" Dovie asked after he'd paid for the robe.

"Please."

They talked a while longer, and then another customer came in and Wade knew it was time to leave. He walked to the town park and sat on a bench, watching the children at play, listening to the sound of their laughter.

Amy had told him about Alex and what had happened once she learned he was married. It wasn't until after she'd broken off the relationship that she'd discovered she was pregnant. Although she'd only mentioned her mother in passing, Wade surmised that they didn't get along and that her mother had provided absolutely no emotional support.

In the days since she'd made her revelations, he'd forcefully pushed all thoughts of Alex and Amy's affair from his mind. It was just too painful to think about Amy loving another man.

He knew that Alex had been afraid she'd come to him and demand child support, so he'd insisted on an abortion. When she refused, they'd had a horrible fight, in which her mother had somehow become involved. She'd also told him, Wade, her mother had come up with an entirely unacceptable suggestion.

Wade could well guess. Six or seven years back, when he worked as a youth pastor in Austin, he'd been approached by a childless couple desperate to adopt a baby. Because of the limited number of available infants and the high number of applicants through legitimate agencies, Wade had been solicited by this couple, who hoped he could arrange a private adoption. They'd made clear that price was no object; in fact, the husband had bluntly spoken of ''buying'' a baby. While Wade appreciated how frustrating such situations could be, he referred the couple to an adoption agency with which he was familiar.

He could only assume that Amy's mother saw her daughter's baby as a profit-making opportunity.

Amy had been calm and collected while she'd relayed the details of her unhappy romance. Too calm, he recognized now. From what Dovie had said, she'd gone to a woman friend the following day and wept bitter tears.

It made Wade wonder why she'd remained so stoic with him. She'd spoken almost as if this had all happened to someone else.

Feeling a strong impulse to straighten things out with Amy, Wade walked over to the feed store. It wasn't the ideal place for such a talk, but this wasn't something they could ignore. They had to have an honest no-holds-barred discussion. And soon. Then he had an idea—he'd invite Amy to dinner. Tonight. At his place so they'd have the privacy they needed.

Never mind that he was absolutely devoid of any cooking talent. Hey, he'd barbecue a couple of steaks, throw some fresh corn in a pot of boiling water. Couldn't go wrong there.

Ellie was nowhere in sight and George was busy with a customer when Wade entered the store. A couple of local ranchers were hanging around the place, as well. Clyde Lester and James Ferguson sat on the front porch drinking cold sodas.

"Afternoon, Reverend."

"Afternoon," he returned, and went in search of Amy. He found her in the back of the store with Lyle Whitehouse. Lyle seemed more interested in talking than in buying. Amy didn't see Wade and he suspected Lyle didn't either. He moved closer, not to eavesdrop on the conversation but... All right, he couldn't help being curious.

"...like to get to know you better," Lyle was saying.

"Thank you, but as I said, this saddle soap is the best one on the market."

Irritation edged her voice. It was all Wade could do not to interfere, but he knew Amy wouldn't appreciate that.

"I noticed you first thing the night of the big dance."

Amy replaced the soap on the shelf. She didn't respond.

"I was thinking you'd be a lot of...fun."

"Is there anything else I could interest you in?" she asked coolly. The minute the words left her lips, her cheeks flushed red. "You know what I mean..."

"Sure thing," Lyle said with a laugh. "And you know what *I* mean."

"If George or I can be of any service, please let us know."

Wade glanced around and wondered what had happened to Ellie; generally, as owner of the store, she was highly visible. He frowned. As far as he knew, Amy had been hired as a bookkeeper, not as a salesperson. He wondered when she'd started dealing with customers and why she hadn't told him about the additional duties Ellie had given her.

"As a matter of fact," Lyle said with a sly grin, "there *is* something you can do for me."

Amy regarded him warily and Wade could see that the ranch hand's proximity made her uncomfortable.

"What's that?" she asked politely.

"As it happens I'm looking for a date Saturday night. Rumor has it you're single."

"I appreciate the offer, but I'm busy."

"Not *too* busy though, right?"

"Yes. Far too busy, I'm afraid."

Amy was about to move away when Lyle placed his hand on her shoulder and stopped her, pinning her against the wall. His oversize belt buckle nudged the mound of her stomach, and Wade felt revolted.

His hackles went up. He couldn't tolerate the idea of any man touching a woman without her consent. As far as he was concerned, Lyle had stepped way over the line. But rather than make a scene, he decided to wait for a few more minutes and let Amy handle the situation herself.

"Ah, come on, Amy," Lyle urged.

"No, thank you."

"What am I missing that the preacher's got?"

"Good manners for one thing," Amy said, trying to get past Lyle. But he held on to her, his grip tightening.

"We could have a lot of fun together," he said. "And once the kid's born you and me could—"

"Let me go!" she demanded.

Wade couldn't remain silent any longer. "I suggest you do as the lady asks," he said, stepping closer.

Lyle snickered and met Wade's look head-on. "What lady?"

Amy closed her eyes as if she'd been physically slapped. Without even knowing what he intended, Wade stormed forward and grabbed Lyle by the shirtfront and half lifted him from the floor.

"I believe you owe the *lady* an apology," he said from between gritted teeth.

"This ain't none of your business, Preacher."

"Wade, please," Amy pleaded.

Wade ignored her. Nose to nose with Lyle, he said, "I'm *making* it my business."

"Is that your bun she's baking in her oven, too?" Whitehouse sneered.

"We're taking this outside, you bastard."

"No!" Amy cried.

"Fine by me, Preacher man. I'll be happy to kick your butt for you."

Wade released him, and Lyle eased his neck back and forth a couple of times. "Anytime, Preacher man," he muttered. "Any time."

"Right now sounds good to me."

"Wade, don't." Amy grabbed hold of him, her fingers digging into his upper arm. "It's all right, please. I don't want you getting hurt on my behalf."

"I can hold my own," he promised her. He turned and followed Lyle out the front door.

Lyle had his fists raised by the time Wade got outside. He squinted his eyes against the bright sunlight as he rolled up his sleeves.

"What's going on here?" Clyde Lester asked.

"Preacher and I have something to settle man to man," Lyle answered.

"Wade, you wanna fight this guy?" Clyde was clearly shocked.

He raised his own fists. "You're damn right I do."

The older rancher looked flustered and unsure. "George," he shouted, "we got trouble here."

George called out to Wade, who turned at the sound of his voice. He didn't even see the fist coming. Lyle's punch hit him square in the jaw. Unable to stop himself, he staggered a couple of steps sideways.

Clyde and his friend cried out that Lyle had cheated. But Wade figured he'd deserved that sucker punch. It would be the last swing Lyle took at him, though.

Wade let out a roar and surged toward Lyle, tumbling them both onto the ground.

Snatches of speech made it into his consciousness. He heard Amy pleading with someone to stop the fight. Clyde was still yelling that Lyle was a cheat. Then George shouted that he was phoning for the sheriff. Soon afterward he heard Lyle grunt with pain. Or perhaps he was the one grunting. Wade didn't know anymore.

High school was the last time Wade had been in a fistfight, but he was strong and agile, capable of moving fast. And he wasn't a coward. Some things were meant to be settled this way, although he generally avoided physical confrontation. But no one was going to insult the woman he loved.

He got in a couple of good punches; so did Lyle. They circled each other like angry dogs and were about to resume fighting when Sheriff Hennessey arrived.

Frank leaped out of his patrol car and stared at Wade as if he couldn't believe his eyes. "What the hell's the problem here?" he said, pulling his nightstick from his belt.

"This is between Lyle and me," Wade said, pressing his finger to the edge of his mouth. His jaw ached, and one eye felt like it was already swelling. Lyle's face looked as if he'd been put through a garbage disposal. Wade figured he didn't look any better.

"Lyle, what happened?" Seeing he wasn't going to get anywhere with Wade, the sheriff tried the other man.

Lyle held Wade's look. "Nothing we can't settle ourselves."

"Well, I don't happen to like the way you two decided to settle it. I could haul you both into jail for disturbing the peace. That what you want?"

"It was my fault, Sheriff," Amy cried, stepping between Wade and Lyle. "Wade thought I needed help…"

Sheriff Hennessey glared at Lyle.

"Were you bothering this young lady, Whitehouse?" the sheriff demanded.

A truck pulled up beside the patrol car and Ellie got out. "What's going on here?"

"Seems like the preacher and Lyle here didn't see eye to eye," Frank explained.

"I didn't do anything but talk to the little lady," Lyle muttered. "Seems the preacher thinks he's got squatter's rights with her. He's—"

"Leave it right there," Frank said, stepping closer to Lyle.

"Are you going to arrest anyone?" Ellie asked.

Frank gave Lyle and Wade a hard look. "Is this over or not?"

Wade narrowed his eyes, which caused him more than a little pain. "If he's willing to let Amy alone, then I'm willing to call it quits."

"Lyle?" Frank focused his attention on the other man.

"All right," he growled, reaching for his hat. He shoved it on his head and stalked toward his truck.

"I think we've seen everything there is to see here," Frank said to the small crowd of curious spectators. He glanced at Wade and his expression said he was disappointed.

Wade wasn't particulary proud of himself at the moment, either. All he'd done was embarrass Amy and himself. He rarely let his temper get the better of him like this. It was a primitive response, he thought grimly. A primitive male response. He'd been in such a rage he hadn't been able to control himself, but damn it all, he was supposed to be an example to the entire community.

"Oh, Wade." Amy gazed up at him with tear-filled eyes. She raised her hand to his mouth.

He winced when her gentle fingers touched the corner of his lips. The taste of blood was in his mouth and his head pounded. His left eye was swollen almost shut.

"I've got a first-aid kit in the back of the store," Ellie said.

Amy and Wade followed her to the office, where she took the kit out of the drawer, then left them. Wade was grateful until he saw the tears running down Amy's face.

"Amy, darling, it doesn't hurt."

Her hands trembled as she tore open a gauze package. "Fighting! Oh, Wade, how could you?"

"I don't know exactly how that happened. Things just escalated. In retrospect, I agree it wasn't the best way to settle this, but I can't change that now."

"I'm perfectly capable of taking care of myself."

"I know, I know." Just then he didn't want to argue the right or wrong of it. He'd much rather Amy held him.

"Sit down," she said curtly. He did, and she dabbed at the cut on his lip. "What do you think people will say when they hear about this?"

"Yeah, well, it can't be helped."

"All I've done is hurt you," she said in a broken whisper.

He wanted to protest, but she touched an especially sore

spot just then. He jerked back from her and brought his finger to the edge of his mouth.

"I think you should see Dr. Jane," she murmured.

"I'm not that badly hurt."

"No, but you need your head examined."

Wade laughed and winced anew. "Ouch! Don't make me laugh." He reached for her hand and held it in both of his. His knuckles were swollen, he noted, and the skin torn. "A kiss would make everything feel better," he told her, only half joking.

Very carefully she bent down and tenderly pressed her lips to his.

The kiss left an ache inside him that made Lyle's brutal punches seem insignificant. He loved Amy. He wanted her for his wife, wanted her to share his life and his bed. He stood up and wrapped his arms around her waist, burying his face in her shoulder.

As she hugged him close, he breathed in her warm womanly scent.

"This can't continue," she whispered, and broke away from him.

Wade wasn't ready to let her go. "What do you mean?"

"I'm hurting you," she said, her voice gaining strength.

She didn't seem to understand the joy and wonder that loving her had given him. He wanted to tell her, but she spoke again.

"Your credibility with the people in your church is going to be questioned because of this fight."

"That has nothing to do with you. I'll deal with that myself."

"Your reputation with the community—"

"Amy, stop."

"No. I won't stop. It's over, Wade, right here and now."

He couldn't believe what he was hearing. "What do you mean, over?"

She seemed to have steeled herself, because she didn't so much as blink. "Over, as in we won't be seeing each other again."

Lyle's sucker punch had surprised him less. "You don't mean that!"

"I do. It was inevitable, anyway," she said.

"What do you mean, inevitable?" He barely recognized the sound of his own voice.

"You and me," she whispered. "I'd need to tell you soon, anyway."

"Tell me *what?*" Although he asked the question, he already knew the answer. Amy had decided to reject his marriage proposal.

"I...can't marry you, Wade."

He sank back down in the chair, crushed by the weight of his pain and disappointment.

"The fact you asked me to be your wife is one of the...the greatest honors of my life. I want you to know that. I didn't make this decision lightly. I've been trying to find a way to tell you all week."

He was a man of words. A man who loved language, who knew how to use it and could respond to any occasion; it was part of his job, of who he was. But Amy's rejection left him speechless. All he felt was an encompassing sadness. And bitterness.

"What about Sarah?" he asked, unable to hide his anger. He felt she was being selfish, putting herself first. He'd offered to be more than her husband; he'd wanted to adopt her child.

"I'll raise her on my own. It was what I intended from the first."

He got to his feet. "You need to do what you think is best."

"That's exactly what I am doing. Thank you," she said, and her voice wavered slightly.

Wade ignored the emotion she revealed and struggled to contain his own. "I apologize for the embarrassment I caused you this afternoon."

"Oh, Wade."

"I won't bother you again." Having said that, he walked out of the office.

Chapter Nine

Preaching Sunday's sermon was one of the most difficult tasks Wade had ever performed during his entire time in the ministry. Word of the altercation between him and Lyle Whitehouse had spread like wildfire through Promise, gathering other rumors and ugly speculations. As he entered the sanctuary Sunday morning, he noticed that he'd drawn a record crowd. The church was filled to capacity, and the overflow had collected in the rear of the room. He'd certainly hoped to pack the pews, but not for a reason like this.

Curiosity seekers had come to see his cut lip and his black eye. They'd come to hear his explanation. He hated to disappoint all the good people of Promise, but he had no intention of offering excuses or justifications. He stood before them as a man who'd made a mistake. One he deeply regretted. He wasn't perfect and didn't pretend to be, but he was ready to accept the consequences of his actions—if it came to that. He hoped it wouldn't, but the choice wasn't his.

The choir opened the service with a favorite hymn of Wade's, written by Fanny Crosby a century earlier. Although it hurt his mouth, his voice joined theirs as he sang, *"This is my story, this is my song..."*

Rather than keep everyone in suspense, Wade approached the lectern when the hymn ended. "Good morning," he said, and managed a painful smile.

His words were enthusiastically echoed back. Several people craned their necks to get a better look at him. It was a wonder Louise Powell didn't topple into the aisle, considering how far she leaned sideways.

Wade didn't blame his parishioners for being curious. His reflection in the mirror told him far more than he wanted to know. He was a sight with his obvious injuries. The swelling in his jaw had gone down, although an ugly bruise remained. If his mother could see him now, she'd box his ears but good.

"Before I begin my sermon," he said, gazing out over the faces he knew so well, "I hope you'll indulge me while I take a few moments to discuss the rumor that I was involved in a fistfight with a local ranch hand."

A low hum of whispers followed.

"What you heard is correct. I was in an altercation this week."

Again he heard whispers, as though his ready admission had shocked certain people, although from his face it should have been obvious that at least some of the rumors were true. "I don't have any excuses or explanations." He cast his eyes down. "As members of this church, you have a right to expect—to demand—that your pastor's behavior be exemplary, above reproach. I have failed you. I've failed myself. I can only offer you my sincerest apology." His hands gripped the podium, his fingers white from the pressure.

"Seeing that such an action might raise a question in your eyes about my suitability as your pastor, I've asked the elders to pass out ballots for a vote of confidence. If you're still willing to have me serve you in the capacity of pastor, then I'll do so with a grateful and humble heart. If not, I'll leave the church. The decision is yours.''

He sat down, and the elders moved through the church, passing out the ballots.

Somehow, Wade managed to finish the service. As soon as he'd given the benediction, he retired to his office while the votes were being counted. Alone with his worries and fears, he tried to imagine what his life would be like outside the ministry. With his emotions muddled, his heart broken and his career badly shaken, Wade desperately needed the affirmation of his church family. Without it...well, he just didn't know.

Max Jordan knocked politely on his office door.

''Come in.'' Wade stood, bracing himself for the news.

Max entered the room and set the ballots on the edge of his desk. ''The vote is unanimous. The members of Promise Christian Church want you to stay on as our pastor.''

Wade sank to his chair in a rush of relief.

''Quite a few of our members have written you notes we thought you should read. You've done a lot for the people in this town, and we aren't about to forget it.''

Wade released his breath in a slow sigh. Even Louise Powell had voted that he stay on. Now *that* said something.

''We're not looking for a saint to lead us, Reverend,'' Max added. ''As you said, what you did was wrong, but you were willing to get up in front of everyone and say so. It's reassuring to know you face the same struggles we do. It isn't always an easy thing, holding one's temper in check. You did the right thing, admitting you'd made a mistake and reminding us that violence isn't a solution.

''Today's the best sermon you've ever preached because we could see you'd reached that conclusion the way we have ourselves. The hard way—through experience.''

Wade nodded, in full agreement.

"We want you to stay, Wade. Each and every one of us."

Wade took hold of Max's hand a shook it. "Thank you," he said.

"No, Pastor, thank *you*."

Wade had never felt so humbled. His congregation had taught him a lesson in forgiveness that he wouldn't soon forget.

DOVIE HAD RARELY SEEN two people more miserable than Amy and Wade. It was clear to her that Amy was deeply in love with Wade and he was equally crazy about her.

"We have to do something," she told her husband early Monday afternoon. Frank generally stopped by the shop at some point for coffee. It was a habit established long before they were married and one she enjoyed to this day.

"You mean about Amy and Wade?" he asked, helping himself to an extra cookie. The peanut-butter cookies half dipped in chocolate were his favorites.

"Who else would I be talking about?" she snapped. She reached for a cookie, too, although she'd recently made a resolution to avoid sweets. But the situation with Amy and Wade had bothered her since Sunday-morning service.

"I don't think I'll ever forget Wade standing up in front of the church and apologizing like that." It'd demanded every ounce of self-restraint Dovie possessed not to leap to her feet and shout that she'd have punched Lyle Whitehouse out herself had she been there.

Wade had offered no justifications or excuses. She knew the details of the fight only because she was married to the town's sheriff. Although Frank hadn't been all that forthcoming.

"I respect Wade for doing that," Frank said. "But we

can't go sticking our noses in other people's business, Dovie, no matter how much we care.''

"But, Frank, this isn't just *anyone*. It's Amy."

Her husband sighed. "I know that, too, sweetheart, but we can't live their lives for them. Amy's old enough to make up her own mind."

"But she's miserable."

Frank hesitated. He and Dovie had grown to love the young woman who'd come into their lives so recently. It was as though they'd been given a daughter to love and cherish. They'd established a closeness that answered needs on both sides; Amy yearned for a family, and Dovie and Frank each had a heart full of love to share. It was almost as though her arrival in Promise had been ordained.

"I love Amy as though she were my own child," Dovie told her husband.

"I know, sweetheart. I do, too."

"Can't we do *something* to help her through this?"

Frank mulled over her question for a moment. "I don't know what we can do other than give her our support."

Dovie sighed, at a loss as to how to help her friend. She longed to wrap Amy protectively in her arms and keep her safe.

Frank left a few minutes later, and she carried their dishes to the tiny kitchen at the back of the shop. Her gaze fell on the beautifully wrapped gift she was holding for Wade. His eyes had shone with emotion—with love for Amy—the day he'd come into the shop and purchased the robe. He'd been almost giddy with happiness—a far cry from the way he'd looked on Sunday.

Amy had skipped church, not that Dovie blamed her. Under the circumstances staying away was probably for the best. Dovie could well imagine Louise hounding her with questions following the service; at least Amy had been spared an inquisition.

On impulse Dovie grabbed the gift and headed out the front door. She turned over the Open sign to read Closed, and walked toward Ellie's feed store with the purposeful steps of a woman on a mission.

Ellie met her out front and waved in greeting. "Hi, Dovie!"

"Is Amy around?" Dovie asked, breathless from her brisk walk. She felt a certain urgency to give Wade's gift to Amy now, despite the fact that it was early afternoon, Amy was at work and she herself had a business to run.

"She's at home." Ellie glanced down at her clipboard.

"She's not ill, is she?" Dovie was instantly concerned.

"I don't think so," Ellie said. She looked up again, meeting Dovie's eyes. "Has she asked you about Bitter End?"

Dovie frowned. "Yes, but not recently." The ghost town wasn't an ominous secret the way it had been in years past, but it wasn't a topic of everyday conversation, either. "What makes you ask?"

"She's been openly curious for some time," Ellie told Dovie. "I might be off base, but she was full of questions this morning, and then she asked for the afternoon off. She borrowed the truck for a few hours, too."

"You don't think she'd actually consider going there, do you?"

"I certainly hope not." But Dovie could tell Ellie was worried.

"When I questioned Amy about her plans, she hedged—as though she didn't want to tell me."

"Then I'll find out myself," Dovie said, and headed toward the small house where Frank had once lived, the gift box tucked under her arm. As she'd expected, Ellie's truck was parked in the driveway.

Amy answered Dovie's knock; her eyes widened when she saw it was her friend. "Dovie," she said, "come in."

Dovie took one look at Amy and instantly knew that Ellie's fears were well grounded. She was dressed in loose-fitting slacks, a sweatshirt and ankle-high boots. "You're going to Bitter End, aren't you?" Amy couldn't very well deny it, dressed as she was. "Amy, for the love of heaven, you can't just go traipsing around the countryside!"

"Why not?"

"Well, for one thing, you're pregnant—and…and it's dangerous."

"Then come too."

"*Me?*" Dovie brought her hand to her throat, taken aback by the suggestion.

"Yes, *you*. You've never been, have you?"

"No," Dovie admitted reluctantly. It wasn't because she didn't want to see Bitter End herself. She did, but Frank had put her off for one reason or another. She didn't think he'd purposely kept her away, just that he believed it wasn't anyplace for her. But she had roots there, too, and was curious about the old town.

"Aren't you interested?"

Dovie had to admit she was. "Even if I was willing to join you, I couldn't," she said. "I don't have any directions…"

"I have a map," Amy said, and led her into the kitchen. "Nell drew it up for me some time ago and I've been studying it."

"You're serious about this, aren't you?" Dovie said, as she gazed at the map.

"Very much so."

"But why now?"

"I...I don't know. I woke up this morning and I felt this...this burning need to do something, go somewhere. I need to get away for a while, I guess. I know it's silly, I know I probably shouldn't, but I want to see Bitter End. I'm prepared to go alone, but I'd rather someone was with me."

It went without saying that if things had been different, Wade would be taking her. Half an hour earlier, Dovie had been looking for a way to help Amy and Wade, and now it came to her that this would offer the perfect opportunity to talk. She and Amy would be spending time alone, and if ever Amy would confide her feelings it'd be now.

"I'll go."

Amy stared at her. "Are you *sure*, Dovie?"

She nodded. "I'll close up for the day, then call Frank and let him know what we're doing."

"He'll try to talk us out of it," Amy said, sounding as though she feared he might succeed.

"I won't let him."

"But..."

"I'll tell you what," Dovie said, thinking fast. "I've got a cellular phone and I'll conveniently forget to call him until we're there."

"Oh, Dovie, are you sure? He might get terribly upset with you."

"I'm sure he will, but Frank needs to know I have a mind of my own," she said firmly. "I've been wanting to visit that ghost town myself." If they were going to find it that afternoon, there were several things she needed to do. First she had to close the shop, then change clothes and leave a written message, as well as pack her cellular. "I'll be back in half an hour," Dovie promised. "Oh," she said, almost forgetting the purpose of her visit. "The package is for you."

Amy glanced at the beautifully wrapped box. "Another shower gift? Dovie, people have been so generous already. I don't know how to thank everyone."

"This isn't a shower gift," Dovie said. "It's from Wade."

At the mention of his name, Amy's head went back as if hearing it brought her pain. "Wade?" she whispered.

"He was in last week—before the fight—and bought it for you."

"But he…"

"He asked me to give it to you after the baby was born."

Amy frowned, obviously wondering why Dovie had brought it to her now.

Dovie shrugged. "I thought you might want to open it."

Amy looked at the box for a long time without moving toward it.

"I'll be back before you know it," Dovie said, suddenly excited by this little adventure. She felt that Amy knew her own limitations; if she wanted to visit Bitter End, then far be it from Dovie to stop her.

AMY LEFT THE PACKAGE sitting exactly where Dovie had left it. But not for long. She couldn't resist knowing what he'd bought, or why Dovie had felt compelled to give it to her now.

She fingered the large pink bow. Dovie had specifically said Wade had purchased the gift for *her*. Not for the baby, but for her.

The look in Dovie's eyes had told Amy something else, too. The gift had been purchased with love. Amy didn't know how to deal with the kind of love she'd found in Promise; it was all so unfamiliar. Frank and Dovie had been incredibly generous and kind. Caroline had become a good friend, and Ellie, in addition to giving her a job, was her friend, too. Dr. Jane had been wonderful, encouraging her, befriending her.

And Wade…

She tried to squeeze out the memory of the hurt she'd seen in his eyes when she said she wouldn't marry him.

She placed the box on her lap and carefully removed the ribbon. When she'd finished peeling away the paper, she set the box on the table, again. She hesitated, afraid that if she opened it, she'd be overwhelmed by a rush of emotion and pain. She hadn't seen Wade since the day of the fight and sincerely doubted she would. He might eventually come to visit her and see the baby, but Amy didn't expect to have more than casual contact with him following Sarah's birth. It hit her then how very much she was going to miss him. How very much she already did. This sudden need to do something, to get out and explore the ghost town, was a symptom of how she'd been feeling since she'd broken off their relationship. Restless, dispirited, lonely. Dovie was right; it was ridiculous to visit the town now, but that wasn't stopping her.

Finally Amy could stand it no longer and lifted the lid. She gasped.

The robe was stunning, beautiful beyond anything she'd ever owned. She put the lid aside and reached for the robe and held it against her. Burying her face in it, she felt surrounded by Wade's love.

She heard Dovie's car just then, surprised it had taken her so little time. Amy glanced out the window and, sure enough, saw Dovie parked in her driveway. She waved, grabbed a sweater and hurried out the front door, map in hand.

"You ready?" she asked.

"Ready, willing and able," Dovie said with a conspiratorial grin.

Dovie drove while Amy navigated. The instructions were clear and it wasn't difficult to find the spot where Nell said to turn off the highway. The terrain was rough after that, but Dovie drove slowly and cautiously, winding around one hill and then another for what seemed forever.

Luckily a number of other cars had followed the same route in recent months, and their tires had worn a narrow path in the hard ground. It seemed incredible to Amy that anyone had ever found this place. They followed the route as far as it took them and stopped by a high limestone ledge.

"This is where the path ends," Dovie said.

Amy continued to study the map. "Nell says we'll need to go on foot from here."

"Down there?" Dovie questioned, sounding unsure.

"Yup," Amy confirmed. She opened the car door and climbed out, then walked to the edge of the limestone outcropping. Nestled in a small valley below was Bitter End. She saw stone and wood structures lining both sides of a main street. A church with a burned-out steeple and fenced graveyard stood at the other end. A corral and livery stable. A two-story hotel. From this distance, the buildings looked intact, as though the years had stood still. Amy sucked in her breath and glanced over her shoulder for Dovie. The older woman came to stand beside her.

"My goodness," she whispered.

The sight was oddly impressive, Amy had to admit. "Let's go see it up close," she said, reaching for Dovie's hand.

Dovie hesitated, studying the rock-strewn descent. "Amy, do you really think we should?"

"I haven't come this far to stop now."

"I know. Should you be climbing down this bluff in your condition?"

"Probably not."

"But you're going to do it, anyway?"

Amy nodded. "We'll help each other."

"If you're sure," Dovie said, and slipped her arm through Amy's.

The trek down wasn't easy. Not with Amy this close to her due date, and Dovie unaccustomed to this type of activity. But they took it slow and easy. Still, by the time they reached the town, both were breathless from exertion and excitement.

"Wow. We're really here," Amy said, taking her first tentative steps into the town.

Dovie's grip tightened on Amy's arm. "Frank would have a conniption if he could see us."

"Let's check it out," Amy said.

"I don't think it's safe to actually go inside any of the buildings, do you?"

"The stone ones look pretty solid," Amy said, surveying the street. This was an absolutely remarkable experience. She couldn't believe she was actually in Bitter End…and only wished Wade was here, too.

Together they explored from one end of town to the other. They identified the old tree, and after some investigation found the word "Cursed," which had been carved into the wood more than a century ago.

"This takes my breath away," Amy said, marveling anew as she traced the letters with her fingertip.

Dovie explained the curse. "I don't think anyone would have understood how this all came about if it wasn't for Nell and Travis. They were the ones to unravel the mystery."

"It's so…" Amy couldn't think of the right word.

''Barren,'' Dovie supplied.

''Exactly.'' Nothing grew in Bitter End. The town and everything around it had died. Bitter End had once held such promise…

Her thoughts skidded to a halt. Her relationship with Wade had been filled with promise, too, but that was dead now too, like this town. *Stop it,* she told herself. *That's a ridiculous comparison.* She was annoyed by her self-indulgence and embarrassed that she'd been so melodramatic. Wade deserved better from her. If only he was here…

As if in protest the baby moved. The pain was fast, sharp, sudden. ''Ooh,'' she said involuntarily, wrapping her arms around her stomach.

''Amy?'' Dovie's voice rose with concern.

''The baby just kicked,'' she said, making light of it.

''You're not in labor, are you?''

''No…no. It's three weeks yet. There's nothing to worry about.'' No sooner had the words left her mouth than warm liquid gushed from between her legs.

Her water had broken.

''Amy, what's happening?''

She heard the panic in Dovie's voice and reached out to take the other woman's hand. ''We have a small problem here,'' she admitted in a shaky voice. ''It looks like no one told Sarah she wasn't due for another three weeks.''

''Your water broke?'' Dovie asked. ''Are you in pain?''

''It's not too bad.'' Amy was more frightened than anything.

''Let's not panic,'' Dovie advised, although her voice was shrill with nerves. She carefully led Amy to the rocking chair outside the hotel and sat her down. ''Let's think this through.''

''All right,'' Amy said, clinging to Dovie's hand.

"Frank. I should call Frank." She said this as if it were divine inspiration.

"What about Dr. Jane?"

"He can phone her," Dovie said. "For now, it's more important that you be comfortable and relaxed."

Amy clasped her abdomen. "I'll be fine as soon as…as soon as this pain passes." She closed her eyes, taking a deep calming breath. After a moment she opened her eyes again to find Dovie gazing at her, lines of worry between her eyes.

"Frank will have my head," she muttered as she punched out the number on the small cell phone and waited. It seemed an eternity before Frank answered. Amy watched Dovie's expression as she explained the situation, then saw her eyes widen. She held the phone away from her ear as Frank's voice gained volume.

"You can yell at me later, Frank Hennessey, but right now there are more important concerns."

The conversation between the two continued, but Amy concentrated on timing her contractions and heard little more of what was said. Dovie started pacing. She'd been off the phone only a minute before it rang, the sound cutting through the still afternoon like a fire alarm. Dovie answered immediately and talked for several minutes.

"That was Dr. Jane," she said when she finished, "but I lost her. My phone's dead. Frank knows exactly where we are, though. He'll see to everything."

Amy was in the middle of a contraction and she closed her eyes, counting the seconds the way she'd learned in class.

"Are you all right?" Dovie asked.

"The pains," Amy whispered.

"They're bad?"

"I didn't think they were supposed to be this intense right away."

Dovie squatted down beside her. "Not to worry. We'll get you to the hospital in Brewster in no time."

"I'm not ready! There's so much to do yet," Amy protested, more confused than frightened. She'd assumed she had three weeks. When she awoke that morning, she'd felt better—physically—than she had in days. But not emotionally. That afternoon she'd experienced almost a compulsion for physical activity. She'd hoped that exploring Bitter End would be an interesting distraction.

Like so much else lately, her adventure had backfired.

"Everything's going to be fine," Dovie murmured.

"I know. It's just that I shouldn't be here... Oh Dovie, how could I have been this foolish?"

"We both were, but everything's going to be fine," she said again. "Frank's on his way and he'll get you to the hospital in plenty of time."

"Thank you," Amy whispered. She closed her eyes to keep her thoughts focused on what was happening to her and the baby. She tried to remember everything she'd learned in the birthing classes, her breathing exercises and the importance of remaining calm and composed. It had all sounded manageable when she was in class; reality was a different matter. She knew she dared not climb back up the steep incline to the car. With her water broken, it could be dangerous for the baby.

Dovie comforted her and counted with her, encouraging her to breathe through contractions.

Finally, what seemed hours later, she heard the sound of someone approaching.

"Thank God," Dovie said. "It's Frank. And Wade."

"Wade?" Amy's eyes flew open. "You knew he was coming, didn't you?" she accused.

"Frank couldn't have kept him away," she said, pleading forgiveness with her eyes. "He was with Frank when I phoned." Dovie regarded her expectantly, as if seeking absolution for not telling her earlier.

"It's all right," Amy said. In truth she was glad he was there. She was afraid and, heaven help her, she needed him at her side.

Wade raced down the hill and into town well ahead of Frank, slowing down only when he reached the hotel steps. His eyes searched hers, his love visible enough that her chest tightened with pain.

"How are you?" he asked.

She smiled. "I've been better."

He clasped her hand in his and kissed her fingers. "I'm coming with you to Brewster. Please don't say no, Amy."

She smiled weakly and nodded. He knelt down in front of her, brushing the hair from her temples.

"Sarah's doing great, I think," she said, gripping his hand.

"What about you? What's the pain like?"

"Like nothing I can describe."

A contraction took hold of her just then and she drew in a deep breath and bit her lower lip. "Oh, Wade," she gasped.

Her hand tensed in his. She didn't mean to be so dependent on him, but now that he was here, she couldn't help it. She needed him. "Count," she instructed. "Please count."

"One, two, three…"

"Slower."

"One…two…three…" He continued until he'd reached twenty and she told him to stop.

She took several big breaths and opened her eyes. "The pains are much more intense than I expected." If they were this strong now, she couldn't imagine what they'd be like later.

"Let's get her to the car," Frank suggested.

"I'm ready," Amy said, and the two men helped her stand. Dovie stepped back and watched, her face taut with concern.

They'd gone only a few feet when another contraction ripped through her, nearly doubling her over. She moaned and clutched her stomach.

"Stop!" Dovie shouted.

"Stop?" Frank repeated, then stared at Dovie. "What's happening?"

"We aren't going to make it to the Brewster hospital in time, not with her contractions two minutes apart."

"What do you mean?" Wade demanded, although her words were perfectly clear.

Frank Hennessey studied him with a shocked white face. "Tell me, Preacher, how much do you know about delivering a baby?"

Chapter Ten

Sheriff Hennessey couldn't have called at a worse time. Max Jordan's pacemaker had gone haywire, and Jane dared not leave him, so she'd sent Frank on to Bitter End with specific instructions to phone the clinic as soon as they arrived in Brewster. The rest of her afternoon had been hectic, with the phone ringing off the hook. When she'd finished sewing up Wiley Rogers's sliced thumb and setting Walt Wilson's broken leg, she sorted through the messages and realized she hadn't heard back from Frank.

She was about to call Brewster Memorial to check when Ellie burst through the door.

"It is true?" Ellie asked, her face bright with excitement as she hurried into Jane's office.

"If you're asking about Amy, yes, it's true," Jane said. She stood in front of her file cabinet and slipped a chart back into place. She felt a rush of excitement herself. "Amy's about to have her baby. It turns out she went into labor in Bitter End."

"Why didn't somebody tell me sooner?" Ellie demanded. "Every tongue in Promise is wagging, and I'm the last person to hear what's happening with my own employee." Disgruntled, she flopped down on the chair and stretched out her legs.

"How'd you find out?" Jane asked, curious. The nuances of small-town life continued to fascinate her. Having been born and raised in Southern California, she never failed to be astonished at the lightning-quick way word traveled in Promise.

"George."

"Who told George?" Jane asked, shaking her head in wonder.

"Pete Hadley, who heard from Denise down at the bowling alley. According to Pete, Denise has a real soft spot for Amy."

A lot of people had a soft spot for Amy, Jane reflected. The young mother-to-be had captured the town's heart. Sunday, when Wade had stood before the congregation and asked for a vote of confidence, the people had given him their overwhelming approval. But their votes hadn't been cast for Wade alone. They were showing support and approval for Amy, as well.

Jane suspected there was even some sneaking admiration over the fact that he'd been defending her against the likes of Lyle Whitehouse. Given the circumstances, a lot of the men in the congregation would have done the same thing.

She didn't think Lyle would be showing his face round town anymore. Billy, the owner of Billy D's Tavern, had suggested the ranch hand take his business elsewhere. Feelings ran high when it came to looking after one of their own. Wade McMillen was highly respected, and folks tended to feel protective toward Amy, too.

"You know who's kind of a gossip?" Ellie said, waggling her eyebrows as if this was an interesting tidbit of information.

"You mean other than you?" Jane teased.

"Me!" Ellie pointed to her chest in mock outrage. "I'm the picture of discretion."

"If you say so." Struggling to hold in a smile, Jane closed the file drawer and waited. "Well, don't keep me in suspense. Who?"

"Martha Kerns."

"The church secretary?" Jane had trouble believing it.

"How else do you think word got around so fast?"

"Hold on here," Jane said, stopping her sister-in-law. "What's Martha got to do with any of this?"

"She was working in the church office when Wade suddenly rushed in and said he was leaving with Sheriff Hennessey."

"Okay, got you," Jane said. It made sense now. Wade had told Martha and word had spread from there. She opened the small refrigerator in her office and removed two bottles of spring water, holding one out to Ellie. "No caffeine," she said.

"Thanks." Ellie reached for it, popped open the top and sank back into her chair. "Do you think Amy's having a boy or a girl?" she asked after a moment of silence.

"Girl," Jane predicted. "After a while a doctor gets a feel for these things. A sixth sense."

"Really?" Ellie sounded impressed.

Jane hadn't a clue which sex Amy's baby was, and as for any measure of shrewd intuition, well, that was a joke. She didn't think she'd be able to carry on this nonsense much longer and abruptly changed the subject. "Have you told Glen you're pregnant yet?"

Ellie leaned forward and set the bottle on Jane's desk.

"From that grin on your face, I'd say he knows."

"He does."

"And he's happy?"

Ellie giggled. "You'd think he was the first man ever

to get a woman pregnant. All this strutting around the house like a rooster.''

Jane shook her head. That sounded just like her brother-in-law.

Although Cal and Glen were brothers, their personalities were vastly different. Jane's husband was quieter, more intense than his fun-loving brother. When she got pregnant herself and the time came for her to tell him, she could predict Cal's reaction. He'd grow quiet, and then he'd gather her in his arms and tell her how much he loved her. He'd pamper and spoil her, and they'd spend long quiet hours making plans for their baby. Glen might pamper Ellie, too, but he'd joke boastfully about it and be sure folks knew what a great husband he was. His high energy and good humor would make him a wonderful father.

"We're telling Mary and Phil tomorrow night," Ellie said.

"They'll be so thrilled." Jane took a long swallow of her drink. "If this keeps up, Promise is going to have a population explosion," she said. First Savannah Smith, then Caroline, Amy and now Ellie. She knew from talking to Nell that she and Travis hoped to add to their family, too. It'd been ten years since Nell had given birth to Emma, but Jane could find no reason for her to experience any difficulty in getting pregnant again. Because Nell was in her midthirties, Travis had voiced his concerns about the risks to her and the baby, but Jane had reassured them.

"Twins run in my family," Ellie said absently.

Jane couldn't help smiling. She could just imagine how her brother-in-law would react to twins.

"Do you think Amy might have had the baby by now?" Ellie asked. She straightened and leaned forward, anxious to hear the latest word.

"I was about to phone Brewster Memorial when you arrived," Jane told her.

"Go ahead. I'd love to be the one to give George the update."

Jane took another drink and flipped through her Rolodex for the phone number.

Just as she'd punched in the number, Jenny entered the office.

"Jane's phoning about Amy," Ellie whispered.

"Oh, good, I was about to ask."

"Dr. Jane Patterson," Jane announced. "I'm calling to check on one of my patients." She asked to speak to the nurse on the maternity floor, then placed her hand over the receiver. "They're transferring me."

"I have a sneaking suspicion Amy's having a boy," Jenny said.

"It's a girl," Jane said confidently.

"Boy," Jenny whispered back.

Jane rolled her eyes and pointed to her small refrigerator. "Help yourself."

"Thanks," Jenny mouthed.

"This is Dr. Jane Patterson from Promise," she said again, launching into her explanation about Amy.

"We're admitting someone now, but I don't have the paperwork yet," the on-duty nurse said. "If you wait, I'll get that information for you."

Once more Jane put her hand over the mouthpiece. "She's arrived safe and sound."

"What took her so long?" Jenny asked, checking her watch.

"Frank probably took extra time not to upset her," Ellie suggested.

Jane frowned. According to her brief chat with Dovie before the cell phone went out, Amy's water had broken and she was experiencing some hard labor pains. She'd expected them to have arrived at the hospital much sooner than this.

"Everything's all right, isn't it?" Jenny asked, her gaze holding Jane's. "They got there okay?"

"With Frank driving, did you have a doubt?" Ellie asked, and drank the rest of her water.

In other circumstances Jane would have traveled with Amy, but that was impossible today. Amy was with Frank, Dovie and Wade McMillen. Unless the mother chose a home delivery as Savannah had, most of the babies in the county were born at the hospital in Brewster.

The floor nurse came back on the line. "What did you say your patient's name was again?"

"Amy Thornton."

"She hasn't been admitted yet," the nurse said matter-of-factly.

"Pardon me?" Jane asked. Although she felt an immediate sense of panic, she remained outwardly calm. "I'm sure there's some mistake. Could you check again?"

"Please hold the line."

Ellie stood. "There's an easy way to settle this. Frank drove in his patrol car, didn't he?"

Jane nodded.

"All we need to do is phone the sheriff's office and ask them to radio Frank."

"Good idea." Jane relaxed while Ellie and Jenny disappeared into the outer room to use the second phone.

The nurse from Brewster Memorial returned to the phone. "I'm sorry, no one in Admitting has talked to or seen anyone named Amy Thornton."

Jane replaced the receiver as Ellie and Jenny appeared in the doorway.

Ellie's face revealed her anxiety. "Something's wrong."

"The hospital has no record of Amy," Jane said.

Jenny chewed on her lip. "I phoned the sheriff's office," she explained, "and they radioed Frank."

"And?" Jane asked.

"There's no response. Apparently he isn't in the patrol car."

"Then where is he?" she demanded.

"That's the problem—no one seems to know," Ellie said. "They've been trying to reach him for the last thirty minutes."

"HOW'S SHE DOING?" Wade asked, unable to hide his anxiety. He no longer cared if Frank or Dovie knew how concerned he was. A rain squall had hit them soon after they'd decided not to carry Amy to the patrol car. They couldn't stay outside with Amy about to give birth; they had to find someplace safe and dry.

Bitter End was the last place he felt was safe for Amy. He blamed himself for this situation; she'd asked him about the town and he'd put her off. He didn't like the idea of her in this dead town, and the thought of her giving birth here sent chills down his spine.

With Amy moaning in pain and Dovie calculating the time between contractions, he felt panic rising inside him. All four of them were already soaked to the skin. The only structure in the town where Amy wouldn't have to lie on the floor was the church with its hard wooden pews, and with the two men supporting her, she managed to make her way inside. There were still some provisions from Richard's stay in the town, including towels, blankets and pillows.

Dovie cleaned a pew while Frank searched for anything

else that might be of use. She and Wade helped Amy onto
the pew, and then Dovie went off to give Frank a hand.
Wade refused to leave Amy's side. He hadn't attended a
single one of the birthing classes, and he didn't know if
he was helping or hindering, but she seemed to want him
there, and God knew he had no intention of leaving her.
Not then. Not ever.

Again and again he counted the seconds as her body
was gripped by contractions. Each one seemed to grow in
length and intensity. He felt as if his heart would break at
the agony she was suffering.

Then Dovie returned with Frank, each of them carrying
a tarpaulin and some other supplies. Rain pounded against
the roof and leaked into the center of the church where
lightning had once struck. It astonished him that the building had survived the wear and tear of the elements all these
years.

"Relax," Frank advised, squeezing his shoulder. "Everything's going to be fine." He'd found a lantern—obviously left there by Richard—and lit it. The immediate
warm glow filled the dim interior.

"I'll relax once I know everything's all right with
Amy," Wade told the other man, too tense to do anything
but worry.

After maybe ten minutes, the rain stopped as suddenly
as it'd come. Wade couldn't remember seeing a cloud in
the sky, and then all at once they'd been trapped in the
middle of a torrent.

Now that they'd made the decision to stay in Bitter End,
it seemed fitting that Amy's child be born in a church,
even one as dilapidated as this. Someone had been inside
recently, and he doubted it was Richard Weston. Probably
Travis Grant. He and Nell were back from their honey-

moon and apparently he'd made a number of research trips to the old town.

"Is everything all right here?" Frank asked nervously. He pulled Wade aside, and Dovie took his place. Amy lay on a pew, a pillow beneath her head and as comfortable as they could make her.

"As far as I know," Wade assured him.

Frank nodded abruptly. "I'll be right back," he said.

"Where are you going now?" Dovie asked.

"To the patrol car. I want to radio the office. Tell 'em what happened and where we are."

"I wish I'd thought to charge the batteries in my phone," Dovie said with an apologetic expression.

"So do I," Frank muttered as he headed out of the church. "I'll get Amy's suitcase while I'm at it. We picked it up before we came out here."

Amy moaned, and Wade knelt down on the floor next to her.

"Oh, Wade, it hurts so much," she whimpered.

"Do you want me to rub your back?" Dovie asked.

"No…no." Amy stretched out her hand to Wade.

He clasped it in his own. Wanting to help as much as he could, he reached for the cool washcloth Dovie had brought in and wiped her brow.

The pain seemed to ease and so did her fierce grip on his hand.

"Have you ever delivered a baby?" Dovie asked him, looking paler by the minute.

"No," he said.

"Me, neither."

"I'm not exactly a pro at this myself," Amy said weakly in what he sensed was an effort to insert a bit of humor. A pain must have overtaken her again because she closed her eyes and started to moan.

"Do something," Wade pleaded with Dovie, who took her position by Amy's feet.

"The baby's fully crowned," Dovie whispered, glancing up at Wade.

Amy's answering smile was weak. "She's coming, Dovie, she's coming." With that she began to bear down.

"Pant!" Dovie instructed. "Pant."

Amy did, and Wade encouraged her with a stream of praise and reassurance.

"The suitcase," Dovie said. "We'll need the suitcase."

"It's in the car," Wade remembered. "Why the hell isn't Frank back? I'll go get it." He loosened his grip on Amy's hand but she refused to release his.

"No! Wade, Wade, please don't leave me."

Wade met Dovie's look.

"I'll go," she said, and hurried from the church.

Wade held Amy's hand against his heart. "I love you."

"I know. I love you, too. So much." Tears slipped from the corners of her eyes and rolled toward her ears. She sniffled once and started to moan again.

"Wade!" she cried. "The baby's coming!"

A calmness came over him, and he moved to the end of the pew, taking Dovie's role. The first thing he saw was a full head of wet dark hair. Amy panted, and the baby's head slipped free. Wade supported the tiny head, which fit perfectly in his large hands. The baby's small eyes were squeezed shut and she didn't look the least bit pleased with this turn of events.

It seemed that no time had passed before Dovie and Frank burst into the back of the church. Frank carried the suitcase.

"We need a baby blanket," Wade called.

Frank knelt down and opened the suitcase, and Dovie rushed forward just as Amy gave a shout and half rose.

As she did, the baby slid into Wade's waiting arms. He gazed down at this perfectly formed miniature human being and experienced such a rush of love and joy it was all he could do not to break into sobs himself.

"Is it a girl?" Amy asked, crying openly.

"No, a boy," Wade said as the infant wailed loudly. The cry pierced through the church and Wade swore it was the most beautiful sound he'd heard in his entire life.

"An aid car's on the way," Frank told them. "I'm going to meet them by the highway."

"Go," Dovie said, and waved him off. She took the baby from Wade and wrapped him in a blanket, then handed the bundle to Wade, while she tended to Amy, who had delivered the afterbirth.

"A boy," Amy said, half sitting to look at her son. Tears streaked her beautiful face.

Tears of his own blurred his eyes as he stared down at the incredibly tiny being. The immediate sense of love he felt for this child was beyond comprehension. It took a real effort of will to hand him to his mother, but at last he laid the baby on her abdomen.

Amy gazed upon her son and lovingly kissed his brow. "Welcome, little Joseph Gair."

The baby screamed, as if he was protesting the rough treatment he'd already received from life.

"Gair—that's my middle name," Wade choked out. It had been his grandfather's first name.

"Your mother told me."

Wade reached out his finger and Joseph immediately clenched it with his hand. The connection was one that would last all his life. Wade was sure of it.

While Dovie finished with Amy, Wade sat at the far end of the pew holding Joseph. The child's eyes opened briefly and he looked up at Wade in the soft light and stopped crying. Within a minute he was sound asleep.

A boy. Not Sarah, but Joseph. "Sleep, darling boy, sleep," Wade whispered, and kissed his brow.

"Is everything all right?" Amy asked, twisting around to see Wade and her son.

"Perfect," he whispered. "Perfect."

Tears glistened in Amy's eyes, and he didn't know how she knew what he was thinking, but she did. He saw it in her look, in everything about her.

"Marry me," he said softly.

"Honestly, Amy, put that boy out of his misery and marry him," Dovie pleaded.

Wade could have kissed Dovie. He'd never been more convinced of anything than the rightness of marrying Amy and making Joseph his son. The moment the infant had entered life, he'd come into Wade's hands—to guide, to love, to support. This was his son, born of his heart. This was the woman he would love and cherish all his life.

"I love you so much," Amy whispered.

"Does that mean yes?"

"Yes." Her whispered response was half laugh and half sob.

This was the way it was meant to be. Amy and Joseph and him, and whatever other children might be born in the years to come.

"The aid car's here," Frank announced from the back of the church.

"Already?" Dovie sounded as though she didn't believe him.

"It was dispatched earlier," Frank said, walking toward them. "Apparently when we didn't show up at the hospital, Jane called the office and they radioed ahead for an aid car."

"It might have helped if they'd arrived ten minutes earlier," Dovie muttered.

Wade knew better. The aid car had arrived right on schedule.

AMY HAD NEVER SLEPT like this. The hospital room was dark, and she sighed and smiled as she reviewed the events of the day before. It didn't seem possible that she'd actually given birth in Bitter End. Things had gone crazy all at once, but she'd always be grateful for the way they'd happened. Otherwise Wade wouldn't have been there, and she couldn't imagine what Joseph's birth would have been like without him at her side.

If she'd ever doubted his love, he'd proved it ten times over in those few hours. She closed her eyes and recalled the incredible sense of rightness that she'd felt when she agreed to marry him. All her doubts and fears had melted away. Instinctively she knew it was what she had to do.

All her reasons for declining earlier remained, but after Joseph's birth, those reasons didn't seem nearly as important. Her greatest fear was that she'd be a detriment to Wade and his commitment to his church. Wade deserved someone better. It was what she'd sincerely felt, but all that had changed when she realized how much Wade loved her and her child. How much she loved him.

Content, she smiled, and for the first time noticed a shadow in the corner. Sitting upright, she saw Wade sprawled asleep in a chair. He'd stretched out his feet and slouched down, his arms flung over the sides.

"Wade," she whispered in astonishment. "What are you doing here?"

He awoke immediately, saw her and smiled softly. Sitting up, he glanced around the room. "What time is it?"

She looked for a clock but didn't see one. "I don't know."

"Oh." He glanced at his watch. "It's 4 a.m."

"Have you been here all night?" she asked.

"Guess so—it sure feels that way." He rubbed the back of his neck and rotated the stiffness from his shoulders.

"You must have been so uncomfortable." Amy couldn't believe that he'd been with her all this time.

"I'll live," he said. "How are you feeling?"

"Starved," she admitted.

He stood and shook out his legs. "I'll see what I can do about scrounging up something to eat."

"Don't go," she begged him, and held out her hand.

He walked over to her side and she lifted her arms to him. They kissed, and it was beautiful, sensual, intense. It felt good to be in his arms again, to recognize that sense of belonging.

"How did you happen to spend the night?" she asked.

She felt Wade's smile against her face. "They let me into the nursery to help with Joseph. I was there, Amy, when they weighed and measured him and washed him for the first time. He doesn't take to baths well." He paused to smile and their eyes held a long moment.

"Oh, Wade, I'm so happy."

"He's a beautiful baby boy," he told her.

"I'm having a little trouble adjusting to the fact that Sarah's a boy!"

"He's got a fine pair of lungs on him, too."

"I heard, remember?"

"Dr. Jane was by, and Ellie and Glen stopped in, too, and there are quite a few floral arrangements. The nurses kept them by their station because they didn't want to disturb your sleep."

"Everyone's been so good to me."

"It's because you're loved."

Amy felt that love. It overwhelmed her that the people of Promise would be this kind. That they would accept a stranger the way they had.

"Everyone was full of questions, too."

Amy could well imagine that.

"I must have been asked a dozen times how you ended up giving birth in the ghost town."

"I guess people think it was foolish of me to go there so close to my due date."

"I don't," Wade countered. "I'm convinced it was exactly where we were supposed to be."

She smiled and understood what he was saying. There was a rightness to her being in Bitter End, as if all this had been ordained long before.

Wade yawned loudly and covered his mouth.

"You must be exhausted," she said.

"I am," he told her. "It isn't every day a man delivers a son and convinces a gal to marry him."

"I should hope not," Amy said, and kissed the back of his hand.

Chapter Eleven

"Dovie," Frank called, hurrying from room to room to search for his wife. He could hardly wait to tell her the latest about little Joe.

"I'm in the garden." Dovie's melodic voice drifted into the house from the backyard.

Frank walked onto the back patio to discover his wife picking ripe red tomatoes from her ever-abundant garden. She wore a large straw hat and, in his view, had never looked lovelier.

"I saw Amy and Joseph this afternoon," he said, and laughed at the immediate flash of envy he read in her eyes.

"Frank Hennessey, why didn't you come and get me?"

"I would have, but it was a chance meeting. I'll have you know that little tyke smiled at me."

"He didn't."

"Dovie, I swear it's the truth. He looked up at me with his big beautiful brown eyes and grinned from ear to ear."

Dovie added a plump tomato to her basket. "He was probably pooping. He's only two months old. That's far too young to be grinning."

"Hey, I'm his godfather. I know these things."

She gave an exaggerated sigh. "And I'm his godmother and I know about these things, too."

"You're jealous because he didn't smile for you first."

"Well, I have news for you, Frank Hennessey. Little Joe most certainly did smile for me." The moment the words left Dovie's mouth, she snapped it closed, knowing she'd said more than she'd intended. Frank recognized that look of hers all too well.

"You've been to see him again," he charged. "I suppose you bought him another toy."

"I didn't," she denied.

The flush in her cheeks claimed otherwise. "All right, all right, I bought him a designer bib. Oh, Frank, it was the cutest little thing you've ever seen."

His eyes narrowed as though he disapproved, but in reality, he was having the time of his life spoiling this youngster, too. Amy and Wade had made him and Dovie the official godparents—and little Joe's unofficial grandparents. Christmas was a month away, and they'd already bought him more presents than Santa delivered to the entire state. They seemed unable to stop themselves. It was as though an entire new world had opened up to them with the birth of this child. They were crazy about the baby and crazy about each other, too.

"The bib was a policeman's uniform complete with badge," Dovie told him. "You aren't *really* angry, are you, sweetheart?"

How could he be? Frank loved this child as though he were his own flesh and blood. He suspected a great deal of this was the result of being present at little Joe's birth, but that was only part of the reason.

Frank had waited until he was sixty years old to marry, and once he'd committed himself to Dovie he wanted to kick himself for leaving it this late. He recalled with clarity the talk he'd had with his wife some months previously.

Dovie had lamented the fact that they would never be grandparents.

He hadn't been much of a churchgoer, but after he'd married, he'd started attending services with her. He remembered one of Wade's sermons about Abraham and Sarah becoming parents well after their childbearing years. In some ways the story reminded him of what had happened to him and Dovie. Amy had arrived in Promise needing a family, and she'd adopted them and they'd adopted her. All the love they had in their hearts was lavished on Amy, Wade and little Joe.

"He's an incredible baby," Frank said.

"Incredible," Dovie echoed.

Frank slipped his arm around her waist. "You're pretty incredible yourself, Dovie Hennessey."

"So I've been told."

He threw back his head and hooted with laughter.

Dovie set her basket of vegetables aside and threw her arms around his middle. Her eyes sparkled with joy as she gazed up at him. "I'm happy, so very happy."

"I am, too." The transition to married life had been much easier than Frank had suspected. He'd fought long and hard, convinced he was too set in his ways to give up bachelorhood—and his stubbornness had nearly cost him the only woman he'd ever truly loved.

Frank hugged Dovie close. "We're going to spoil that baby rotten!" he declared.

"But, Frank, we're going to have so much fun doing it."

Frank could see that once again his wife was right.

THREE MONTHS after Christmas Savannah Smith ventured into Bitter End. What she found caused her to race back to the ranch and breathlessly inform her husband. Laredo suggested she tell Grady and Caroline that same afternoon, which she did. The news burst from her in a rush of excitement.

"You're sure about this?" Grady asked.

"Grady, I know what I saw."

Caroline and five-month-old Roy came to visit the following day. "You went to Bitter End?" her best friend asked. "Good grief, Savannah, what would ever make you go back there?"

"The anniversary of my first visit. It was two years ago, March twentieth, and I wanted to see if the rosebush I'd planted in the cemetery had survived."

Savannah's whole life had changed that day two years earlier when she found a weary cowboy walking down the side of a country road and offered him a ride. She'd never done anything like it before and she never would again. For the first and only time in her life, she'd picked up a hitchhiker, and before the year was out she'd married him. She and Laredo Smith had become partners in the Yellow Rose Ranch and partners for life.

"Grady phoned and told Cal," Caroline said, cradling her son in her arms.

"I talked to Nell and Travis, too," Savannah said.

"Someone must have phoned and told Wade."

"Glen and Ellie, I think," Laredo suggested.

"Wade suggested we all meet out there first thing in the morning."

"You're going, aren't you?" Caroline asked.

Laredo and Savannah looked at each other and nodded. "We wouldn't miss it," he told her.

Fourteen of them planned to gather in the ghost town and see the strange phenomenon for themselves. Each one had been to the town at some point or other in the past two years. Each for his or her own reasons.

Savannah felt a certain responsibility to be present, since she was the person who'd started it all two years ago when she'd gone to Bitter End in search of lost roses. She was also the person who'd stumbled upon this latest wonder.

They met and parked their vehicles outside the town. Then each couple walked down the steep incline onto the dirt road that led into the center of town.

Savannah watched and smiled at their reactions, knowing that the same sense of astonishment must have shown on her face twenty-four hours earlier.

Grady's arm was around Caroline's shoulder. Roy was asleep in his carrier. Little Joe, too. Savannah knew that in the years to come these two boys would be best friends. Much the same way Grady and Glen and Cal had been from grade school onward.

"It's true," Ellie whispered. Her pregnancy was obvious now. Glen's hand held hers.

"It's a miracle," Nell whispered, gazing around her.

All around them, in every nook and cranny, against the corral, by the old water trough and even near the large rock, roses bloomed. Their scent wafted about, perfuming the air, their muted colors bringing life and beauty to a once dead place. Pansies winked from small patches of earth—gardens a century ago—and bluebonnets covered the hillside, waving bright blue petals in the breeze.

Perhaps most incredible of all was the dead tree in the center of town. Up from the trunk had sprung new life, green shoots. In time the new tree would overshadow the old; life would vanquish death.

"Who can explain such a thing?" Frank asked, awe-struck.

Savannah understood his awe; she felt the same way herself. Naturally there'd be a logical explanation for what had happened if they sought one. Most likely a freshwater spring had broken free.

"I don't know that I can explain it," Travis said, looking thoughtful. "But I can speculate about what might have caused this."

Everyone turned to him. "Bitter End's come full circle now," he said.

"Why now?" Ellie wanted to know.

"Well, keep in mind that I'm a writer—a storyteller—and I like events to have a structure. I like a sense of completion." Travis smiled at Amy and Wade. "But if my guess is right, we have little Joe to thank for all this."

"Joe?" Amy gazed down on her sleeping son.

"Amy, too," Dovie added, slipping her arm around the young mother's waist.

"A preacher's son died in Bitter End all those years ago," Travis said. "And now a preacher's son has been born here. So, like I said, everything has come full circle."

"Full circle," Savannah whispered, knowing instinctively that this was indeed what had happened.

"The curse is gone."

Savannah smiled. "And in its place is a profusion of beauty."

A town in bloom, filled with promises for the future. Promises for life.

Dear Friends,

Lone Star Baby wraps up the Sons of Promise series. Everything's coming up roses in Bitter End, and Promise is about to experience a population explosion. My stubborn cowboys have all met their matches in love and in life. I'm sorry to leave my friends in Promise behind, but…new friends and adventures are beckoning me.

No project this involved can be accomplished without a lot of help from quite a few talented people. First and foremost, my editor, Paula Eykelhof. No writer works with a better editor than I do. Paula has my unfailing devotion for the long hours she put into every stage of Sons of Promise. Again, I was fortunate to have Maryan Gibson as copyeditor on this series. Andrea Szego, editorial assistant, was an invaluable asset to both Paula and me. And proofreader Peter Cronsberry, who expertly read through the entire Midnight Sons series, also worked on Sons of Promise. Rick Lovell painted the beautiful cover illustrations, and Lorraine Paradowski was the creative art editor on this project. Thanks to everyone for a terrific job!

Only the author's name appears on a book cover, but I

wanted you to realize that no author stands alone, and the team I work with is the best!

As ever I love to hear from readers and you can write to me at P.O. Box 1458, Port Orchard, Washington 98366.

Thank you again for joining me in Promise. Hope you enjoyed the visit!

Warmest regards,

Debbie

MILLS & BOON®

Medical Romance™

COMING NEXT MONTH

MORE THAN A MISTRESS by Alison Roberts

Anna's first House Officer job was in surgeon Michael Smith's hospital. She couldn't believe this was the same man she'd met on holiday, and parted from so badly. And Michael was no happier to see her!

A SURGEON FOR SUSAN by Helen Shelton

Susan was appalled when her sister set her up with a blind date! But Adam had been equally set up, by *his* sister. He was *so* gorgeous, why would anyone think he needed help finding a woman?

HOME AT LAST by Jennifer Taylor
A Country Practice—the third of four books.

After a year away Holly Ross felt able to come home. Many changes awaited her, not least a new stepmother. But the biggest change of all was her growing feelings for Dr Sam O'Neill, the partnership locum.

HEART-THROB by Meredith Webber
Bachelor Doctors

Peter's photo was plastered on *Hospital Heart-throb of the month* posters, embarrassing him when Anna came to work with him in A&E. She was intriguing and mysterious, and Peter couldn't help being fascinated. But he'd managed to stay a bachelor this far...

Available from 2nd July 1999

Available at most branches of WH Smith, Tesco, Asda, Martins, Borders, Easons, Volume One/James Thin and most good paperback bookshops

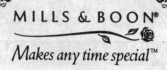

THE Regency COLLECTION

Where rogues find romance

Look out for the third volume in this limited
collection of Regency Romances from
Mills & Boon® in July.

Featuring:

Dear Lady Disdain
by Paula Marshall

and

An Angel's Touch
by Elizabeth Bailey

Still only £4.99

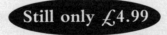